HOMECOMING

THE CRANE DIARIES 1

BY APRYL BAKER

HOMECOMING

Limitless Publishing, LLC
Kailua, HI 96734
www.limitlesspublishing.com

Formatting: Limitless Publishing

ISBN-13: 978-1-64034-433-4
ISBN-10: 1-64034-433-0

DEDICATION

For Challis Payne
I admire you for standing up for yourself
in the face of bullying and never letting it
get you down.
You are an amazing young lady.

1

"You're insane."

I've heard worse. But maybe he's right. Maybe I am insane. Why else would I be on the roof of a house trying to talk a ghost down? He's already dead, so why am I trying to talk him out of jumping?

Because he needs to move on, that's why. And that *is* my job. I'm a living reaper. I convince ghosts they need to move on and stop haunting the living. It never works out well. I mean, if they stay here long enough, they'll go crazy and start hurting people. That's something we don't want.

Now, if only Kane will shut up and let me work, we'll all be fine.

The guy can't be more than eighteen or twenty. Red hair, his white face splattered with an abundance of freckles, and he's tall. Freakishly tall, basketball player tall, but really thin, giving his face more of a hawk-like look. The determined way he's staring at the ground below him makes me crawl along the shingles faster. If I don't reach him, I'll have to come back tomorrow and try again.

"Hey, you!" I shout, knowing I can't startle him into falling. "You there, about to jump off the roof."

At first, he doesn't even respond, but after a moment, he turns his head and looks at me. Blue eyes watch as I finally make the last few feet of the roofline to where he's standing.

"Why are you still up here jumping off the roof?" I stand, my legs a little shaky.

He looks from me to the ground below him, frowning. I think I confused him.

"I'm Emma." I inch closer. "I'm here

to help you."

"Nobody can help me." His voice is flat, toneless, but it carries the scratchiness of the dead. It's a sound that always slithers along my spinal cord and makes me shiver.

"Yes, I can." I inch a little closer until I'm standing beside him, looking down at the ground. Jeez, it's high. One good wind, and I could easily fall. Or the ghost guy could get annoyed and push me. I'm not discounting either option.

"No." The guy shakes his head. "There is no help for me. I only have one option left."

"To jump. I know." I take a deep breath, steeling myself against the cold creeping into my bones. "You already did that. A long time ago."

The ghost shakes his head, anger starting to bleed into his fathomless blue eyes. "Go away."

"Sorry, can't. I need you to understand you're already dead so I don't have to come back tomorrow. I have plans."

"What are you talking about?"

3

"What's your name?"

"Steve." His frown deepens. "Why won't you go away and leave me alone?"

"Because I'm a reaper, and my job is to make you understand you don't belong here anymore. You already died, and your ghost is stuck here, repeating your death over and over every day at this exact same time."

"You're crazy."

Sometimes it would be easier if I were crazy.

I turn around, my back to the ground, and ignore Kane's warning shout from below. He's supposed to be my trainer in all things reaping, but most days he's yelling at me not to take so many chances. Yada, yada, yada.

Closing my eyes, I focus on the most loving memories I have. I think about warmth and joy, and before I know it, the softest glow bathes my closed eyes. There it is. Sure enough, a glowing yellow haze has appeared before us, growing until it's an opening into the very air around us. The other side.

4

"See?" I toss the ghost a grin. "There's the light. You don't have to stay here, jumping and dying every day for an eternity. You can move on, find your family, be at peace."

"What is that?" he whispers, taking a step closer. All ghosts inherently want to move on, but sometimes they can't for whatever reason.

"The next life?" I make it a question, because honestly, I'm not really sure. I know he'll be ferried through the Between, the plane between this world and the afterlife, and then be judged. I don't tell him that little fact. I'm guessing he's still here because he feels guilty about killing himself.

"Who are you?" He takes another tiny step closer to the light.

"I'm Emma Rose Crane."

"I…Jason?" He squints, looking into the light. Most ghosts will see the reapers who come for them as someone important to them, usually a family member who has died. Parents, grandparents, siblings. Or sometimes childhood friends.

"Who's Jason?" I shuffle along with him. I can't force him to go into the light. He has to do it himself, but I can try to persuade him all I want.

"My cousin. He died when we were kids."

Bingo. "See, Jason's there waiting for you. He doesn't want you hurting anymore. There's no reason for you to keep jumping to your death."

"What are you talking about?" He turns to face me, confusion stamped all over his face. "I would never kill myself."

"But I've seen you jump from this roof every day for the last week at exactly the same time."

"No, I didn't. I wouldn't. We don't believe in that."

This doesn't make sense. I've seen him jump myself. "Then why are you up here on the roof, Steve?"

"I was thinking about stuff. It's where I come to be alone."

"Stuff?"

He sighs but inches closer to the light. "I want to tell my family about Mark, but I don't know how they'll react."

Ohhhh, he's afraid of telling them he's gay. Is it possible he fell by accident? That he came up here to think and accidentally went off the roof? Makes sense, I guess.

"I promised Mark I'd tell them, but I don't know how. My dad…he's not going to take it well at all. He's hardcore religious."

"Steve." I lay a gentle hand on him. He's still full of energy, probably not long dead. If this was his house, his family must have moved. It's empty now. "You don't have to tell them anything anymore. You're dead."

"I'm not dead. I was just talking to my sister a few minutes ago."

"Look around." I sweep my hand at the empty landscape. "The house is empty, there are no cars here except for mine. No one lives here anymore. You died, and they moved on. Now it's your turn to move on. Jason's waiting for you. All you have to do is step into the light."

"I'm really dead?" He shuffles closer until he's almost touching the light. He's not looking at it, though. His eyes are sweeping the abandoned farmhouse's yard, listening for sounds that aren't there anymore.

"What year is it?"

"Two thousand one." He frowns, watching the cellar door bang against the opening in the wind. "Where is everyone?"

I pull out my driver's license. I'd shoved it in my pocket since I refuse to carry a purse, much to Mary's disgust. "Here, look. It's 2018. You've been dead for a long, long time."

"I…" He trails off, staring at the date on my ID, horrified.

"You've been reliving this moment every day since then, but you don't have to anymore. All you have to do is step into the light and move on. People who love you are waiting for you."

Kane pops onto the roof beside me, startling both Steve and me. I hate when he does that.

"She's right, you know. I can take you through the light if you're afraid."

"I…who are you?"

"This is Kane. He's a reaper."

"Reaper?" Steve backs away from us, and I want to beat Kane. I almost had the kid into the light. Then Kane had to go scare the crap out of him.

"Easy, Steve." I keep my voice calm and very Officer Dan, like when he's trying to soothe me. "Kane is one of the good guys. It's his job to ferry lost souls to the other side, to where Jason is waiting for you."

"But…I…I can't be dead. It's not fair. I'm only sixteen…and Mark…oh, God, Mark. What about Mark?"

My heart breaks a little for him. He sounds so lost and forlorn. It's hard for some ghosts to accept they're dead, especially ones who died unexpectedly.

"I'm sorry, Steve, but you *are* dead. Mark isn't sixteen anymore. He's moved on, and it's time for you to do the same. Let Kane take you to Jason where you

9

can be happy. There will be no fear or worry on the other side. You'll be loved and accepted and among family."

Kane holds out his hand. "It's going to be okay. I promise."

Steve eyeballs Kane's outstretched hand for the longest time before hesitantly placing his hand in the reaper's. "I…are you sure I'm dead?"

"I'm sure." Kane grips the teen's hand tighter. "But it's okay. Everything is going to be just fine. It's time to go."

Steve's face scrunches up, but he doesn't refuse. Instead, he follows the reaper into the glowing doorway that's standing open between this plane and the next. He gives me one more solemn look and steps into the light. The bright rip in the fabric of the planes closes behind them, and I let out a deep breath.

Steve was like most ghosts, shocked to learn they're dead, but at least it hadn't taken me hours to convince him. The last ghost I helped, I sat with her for over three hours trying to talk her into believing she was dead. I might actually get some stuff done today…crap.

I check my watch and start scrambling toward the ladder. I was supposed to pick Mary up fifteen minutes ago. She's going to kill me. Getting into my car, I take off for the Tulane campus, hoping she won't be too angry.

Thank God for speech to text. I shoot Mary a quick message telling her I am on my way. It takes me about half an hour to get back into the city of New Orleans and onto Tulane's campus. It never fails to shock me how gorgeous the campus is. It showcases the culture and history of the city. There's this massive oak tree with benches under it that I'd discovered. It's my new favorite spot to sit and draw. The oak inspires me in ways I can't even begin to describe. The buildings are beautiful, the almost gothic architecture another big inspiration in my drawings.

I park in our designated parking area.

Greenbaum House is one of the two newest dorms on campus. We have a suite with our own bathroom instead of having to share one with every resident on our floor. A shudder rolls through me just thinking about that. One of the nice things about having a dad who can afford whatever he wants is I get a decent dorm. He made sure Mary and I shared the bathroom, and we didn't have a roommate in our connecting rooms. Not sure if Zeke had to pay double the room and board, but I am grateful.

If it had been left up to Zeke, Mary and I would still be living with him and being chauffeured to classes. Not that I blame him. It took us a year to recover after the events in Charlotte, North Carolina. Mary had been taken hostage by a Fallen Angel, and I'd shattered my soul to save her. We were both still in therapy for that, but we wanted to try normal again. Mary still isn't the same person she used to be, but she's slowly starting to come back from it. She smiles more and more, but the haunted look in her eyes may never completely go away. I don't know what happened to her. She won't talk about it with me, but she knows I'm here whenever she's ready.

We'd chosen the new dorm not only because of the nicer rooms, but because we figured it would be less haunted than some of the older buildings. Ghosts tend to find me, and it's easier to not invite every resident haunting within shouting distance into our rooms. My undead visitors can wake Mary up too. She hears ghosts, thanks to her out-of-body experience a few years ago.

That's how my sister and I met. I'd grown up in foster care, not knowing I had a dad who spent every waking moment looking for me. My mother, who I found out stole me from my parents, tried to kill me when I was five. I'd died but had been brought back, thanks to the EMS people, but it woke up my reaping abilities, and from that moment on, I could see ghosts. A curse and a gift.

Anyway, Mary had been kidnapped and tortured so much, her soul left her body and came to find me, as many ghosts do. I knew she wasn't dead, though, and Officer Dan Richards and I set out to look for her. Only I got ahead of myself and ended up being kidnapped and tortured myself. The serial killer, as we discovered she was, turned out to be my then-foster mother, Mrs. Olson. With the help of several ghosts, including my Mirror Boy, we'd escaped, and Mrs. Olson had been arrested. She'd been committed, so there wasn't any trial we'd had to suffer through. We'd met as strangers and came out sisters. You don't survive what we did and not come out the other side as family.

Yawning, I turn off the ignition and get out of the car. Mary texted me back to say she'd meet me in the dorm. I can definitely go for a nap if she doesn't want to drag me along on whatever adventure she's been rattling on about since this morning.

I take the stairs up to the third floor. Not because I'm trying to stay fit, but because I've had so many bad experiences in elevators. Ghosts like to take control of the elevator and force me to the deepest, darkest part of the building. I avoid elevators now whenever possible. Keeping myself in shape is just an accidental bonus.

My room is a mess. Clothes litter the floor, and art supplies take up every other surface in the room, except for my bed. I don't think I've made my bed in a few days. I can hear Mrs. Cross, Mary's mom, nattering away in my ear about making my bed. It was a pet peeve of hers, and I *had* tried to remember to do it, but, well, why make it when you were just going to get back into it and mess it up again? My logic drove her crazy.

"Mary!" I glance at my watch. I'm so late.

My sister comes hurtling through the bathroom, ready to murder me. She's wearing jeans and a dark t-shirt, her blonde hair pulled back in a high ponytail.

"Where have you been?" she demands, looking around at the mess that is my room. Her room? Neat and tidy. We are as different as daylight is to dark. "Seriously, Em, you need to at least use the laundry basket. Stuff is probably growing under all this by now."

She refuses to call me Emma Rose. She knew me as Mattie Hathaway, and to her I'll always be Mattie. But being Mattie brought me nothing but pain. I want to try being Emma Rose, the girl with people who love her and not the freak foster kid.

"Eh, it'll keep until the weekend. I'm going to wash everything then. So, what's the big hurry? You said I needed to be here as fast as I can."

"And you're late." She gives me the stink eye, though her blue eyes are more agitated than irritated. Something's definitely up.

"I was helping a ghost. Didn't know he was dead." I collapse on the bed.

Mary sighs but stops complaining. "What happened to him?"

"I thought he was a jumper, but I think he fell off the roof by accident."

"Aw, that's awful."

"Yeah." I feel bad for the kid, but at least he's found peace now. "So, what was so urgent you made me break the speed limit?"

Mary rolls her eyes, knowing good and well I did no such thing. I'm doing my best to stay out of trouble down here. I want no one to know about my rap sheet back in Charlotte. The police and I have a rocky past. Zeke is quite proud of it, as he himself partakes in criminal activities. Not that he tells me about his adventures, but I've seen his file. I haven't read it, but I've seen how thick it is.

"I met a guy."

That makes me sit up. This is the first time since we left Charlotte she's shown any interest in a guy. The last guy she liked was Caleb Malone. My mind skitters away from thoughts of the Malones. It brings back memories I'm still not ready to deal with.

"A guy?" I try to keep my voice casual instead of super excited. She's been so reserved and quiet, I don't want to scare her.

"His name's Wade, and he invited me to come help him out this week."

The very hesitant way she says that sets off alarms. "Help him with what?"

"Well…" She starts picking at the bottom of her t-shirt, refusing to look at me. "He runs a paranormal investigation group. They have their own YouTube channel and everything."

Paranormal investigation group?

"Mary, please don't tell me you've gone and gotten yourself involved in some kind of ghost hunting nonsense."

"It's not nonsense. You and I both know better."

"Mary…"

"Just hear me out, okay?" Her baby blues plead, and I groan, nodding. It's freaking hard to say no to her.

"I like Wade, and I've been talking to him for about a month now. He told me all about him and his friends and how they go out and investigate haunted places around New Orleans. They have over a hundred thousand followers on

YouTube."

Great. A YouTuber seeking fame and fortune using cheap tricks and illusions to mimic hauntings.

"Do I think he has any clue about actual ghosts? No, but he thinks he does and wants to bring me along on their newest location to show off what he does."

"Do I hear a 'but' in there?"

"I don't want to go by myself. I know Wade, but I don't know his friends. I want someone else there in case I stupidly misjudged him and…"

"And you need to kick some butt?" I finish for her. Mary isn't stupid. Going off on her own was how she'd fallen into Mrs. Olson's hands to begin with.

"Yeah." She smiles hesitantly, still picking at her t-shirt hem. She looks a little lost. It's the first time she's shown any interest in boys since her year-long captivity at the hands of Deleriel. No way am I not supporting this. It's the first real sign she's getting better.

"I got your back." Pulling my phone

out of my pocket, I text Eric and tell him to get his butt over to my dorm. "We're bringing Eric too."

"Let me tell Wade I'm bringing friends." She turns and runs back to her own room, more excited than I've seen her in a long time.

My phone rings, and I answer it, knowing who it is. "Hathaway, what's up?"

Leave it to Eric, who often forgets I left everything to do with Mattie Hathaway behind in Charlotte. But that's not true, though. Eric is a part of the past I wanted to escape, but I can never leave my Mirror Boy behind.

"We're going ghost hunting."

"What?" It sounds like whatever he's drinking spewed out of his mouth.

"You heard me. Now, get over here. We're already late." I don't give him time to argue, just hang up the phone.

Mary skips back into the room— actually *skips*. "Wade says it's cool if you guys come. Does this outfit look okay for ghost hunting? Well, not actual ghost hunting. Today is the interview stage."

"Interview?"

"He has to interview the family that lives there, get information and all that. You should know this since you're the *Ghost Adventures* junkie."

"It's *research*, Mary, research." Truthfully, I just like the show. There are some creepy moments that really are unexplainable. Most of those shows are junk, but it's the only one I'll give any credit to.

"Uh-huh." Mary stares pointedly at my shirt, and I look down. A long yellow stain smears the front of it. The hot dog I grabbed for lunch. I hope to God no one noticed it in class. My luck, though, they did. Dang it.

"Don't worry, I'm changing."

Mary goes back to her room while I start rummaging around in what little clean clothes I have left. This is definitely going to be an interesting afternoon. Chances are there are no actual ghosts, and everything can be explained, but then again, you never know.

Either way, we'll know soon enough.

3

Jacob Eric Owens. My Mirror Boy.

The ghost in the mirror that nearly killed me the first time we met.

He ended up saving me not once, but twice. I reaped his soul to defeat a ghost that was killing me. I thought he was gone forever until Jake Owens, my ex-boyfriend, was shot by his psychotic brother. When I went to see Jake in the hospital, I knew his soul was gone. He was just an empty shell. The reaper in me sensed it, and I had an idea. When I reaped Eric's soul, it stayed with me, and there sat Jake's empty body. Why not transfer Eric's soul into it? I didn't know if it would work or not, but I tried, and to my amazement, it did.

For once, the powers that be didn't chastise me for using the gifts I was given. Eric got a family who would love him forever, and Jake's parents got their son back. The doctor's told them he had amnesia, and they accepted the Jake they knew may never come back, but they'd love the new Jake as much as they did the old one.

He's leaning against my car when Mary and I emerge from our dorm. Spiky brown hair and eyes so blue they can make the cloudless sky weep from envy greet us. He takes no notice of the girls ogling him. It only makes them want him more.

"Hathaway, I was on a date."

It's still unsettling to hear Jake's voice when Eric speaks. I'm not sure I'll ever get used to it.

"It couldn't have been much of a date if you're here instead of there." I unlock the car and get in.

Eric beats Mary to the front seat. She

shoots him an annoyed look but doesn't argue. She leans between the seats and programs the GPS. I'm not familiar with the area she's plugged in. Even though we've been in New Orleans for over a year, I haven't explored it as much as I want to. Neither of us was in any shape to leave the house for the first few months, and after that, I just didn't want to deal with the random ghosts.

"She was cute enough, but I was starting to get bored." He turns the radio on, slapping Mary's hand when she tries to lean forward and change the channel. "Seatbelt!"

She rolls her eyes but buckles up. "Which girl was it this time?"

He slouches at her question. "Just a girl from my English lit class."

"The redhead?" Mary checks her phone, her tone idle, but I know better. She's digging for information.

"Maybe."

"So, why were you bored? If it's the redhead, I know her. She's smart and funny."

"Can we drop it?"

"Why do you want to drop it?" Mary pushes herself as far forward as the seatbelt allows. "Maybe because you really want to ask out the guy in our physics class? The hottie with the phoenix tattoo?"

His face flames up, and I barely suppress a laugh. Eric woke up in Jake's body with a newfound sense of how hot the guys around him are, much to his dismay. Eric was straight before he died, but Mary and I both think Jake wasn't. Since Eric is now in Jake's body, he inherited certain tendencies, from Jake's deep and abiding love of fried pickles to his closet sexuality. Eric has not been handling it well.

"Shut up, Mary." The low growl that emits from him doesn't deter her.

"It's not like anybody cares who you like or who you don't. We just want you to be happy."

"So, harassing me about…about *that* is making me happy?" He turns to look out the window, ignoring her.

"I've never had a brother before, and from what everyone tells me, it's mandatory for the big sister to harass her irritating little brother."

That gets his attention. He turns around in his seat and looks at her, his eyes unreadable. "You think of me as your brother?"

"Of course. Same as Em is my sister. The three of us, we're family."

I know what he's thinking. Mary will never be able to understand what those words mean to a foster kid. We grew up, shuffled from one home to another, never having anything permanent. What she's offering him is more precious than any material thing he'll ever possess. Family, love, acceptance. Mr. and Mrs. Owens are great, but they love him, thinking he's Jake. Mary's offering him acceptance as *himself*, even if that comes with calling him on his nonsense.

"Thank you, Mary."

She shrugs, her smile lighting up her face. "Just don't embarrass me in front of Wade."

"Wade? Who's Wade?"

"He's the one who invited us on the ghost hunt." She types a quick message on her phone. "So, be nice."

"Do I need to be all brotherly?" he asks, his eyebrows diving down into a severe frown. His attempt to look serious. Uh, not so much. He looks like he's in need of a bathroom instead.

"God, no. Just…just be normal."

I let out a chuckle at this. None of us are normal.

"Well, as normal as we can be," Mary amends when she hears me laughing.

"So, ghost hunting?" Eric settles back into his seat and focuses on me. "Are you going along to see if there are ghosts roaming around?"

"Nope. I'm going because Mary didn't want to go by herself. They don't know what…wait, they don't know about me, do they?"

"Of course not. I didn't tell him I can hear ghosts either." Mary rolls her eyes like we should realize she wouldn't be spilling family secrets to strangers.

"Are they some kind of club you joined or something?" Eric yawns.

"No. Wade has his own YouTube channel about paranormal investigations he's done."

"Great. A wannabe YouTuber who thinks they're gonna be the next big star." Eric can't hide his disgust any more than I could.

"He's got over a hundred thousand subscribers." Mary sounds defensive, and I shoot Eric a warning look. He's not going to ruin this for her.

"Are you sure this is the right place?" The GPS is announcing we'll reach our destination on the right any second now. It's not at all what I expected. We're in one of the nicer neighborhoods near the Garden District, not the rundown, abandoned places that look haunted closer to the outskirts of town. Kids are playing in well-kept, manicured lawns like there's not a worry in the world. Not your usual hotspot for a ghost.

The house is a ranch style brick home with large white columns gracing the front porch entrance, giving it more of that Creole character the city is famous for. There are lots of windows, and the roof looks new. A yellow tricycle rests upside down on the lawn. A black Toyota Tundra sits in the driveway next to a new Ford Focus. An older looking Honda is parked behind them, and I pull in next to it. A van is idling on the sidewalk in front of the house. The garage door is down, and I wonder if there's another vehicle hiding from the heat in there.

It looks lived in and well cared for. The poor people are probably hearing pipes or something groan in the night.

"I know I haven't been a ghost in a while, but this is not one of our usual hangouts." Eric gets out and eyeballs the place skeptically. "This is swanky."

Compared to some of the places he and I lived, this *is* a swanky place, even though it's probably considered your average middle-class home. Mary lived in a place like this growing up.

Doors opening and closing catch our attention. Three guys pile out of the van

I'd noticed earlier. The grin on Mary's face tells me the one hurrying over is Wade. He's not bad looking. Brown eyes and dishwater blond hair cut to look messy. I can barely stop the eye roll. The boy is trying too hard. Eli pulled off that same look effortlessly.

And just like that, a wave of grief hits so hard it almost cripples me. He's been gone a year now, and I still can't think about him without feeling like all the air around me turns stale and thin. It hurts so much.

Eric slips an arm around me, knowing without even asking what's wrong. I lean into him and watch Mary greet her new crush. It helps to ease the sudden pain clenching my heart.

She's gushing, a sure sign she's invested.

"You okay, Hathaway?" His breath tickles my ear. I used to have a crush on Eric. He'd kissed me on my birthday when he was still a ghost. He'd body jumped a guy to be able to do it. Eli and Dan changed all that for me. Eric is just

32

Eric now, my best friend in the entire world. There are no feelings there aside from friendship.

"It's his hair. It just took me by surprise."

"Eli rocked it better." Eric gives me a squeeze. "Mary's really into this guy, huh?"

"Yeah, so be nice. This is the first time since…" I break off, as unable to talk about it out loud now as I was back then.

"I'm always nice."

This earns him my best death stare. "Do we need to remember Sean from therapy?"

"He was a creeper hitting on both of you. Turns out I was right too. They admitted him after he went all stalkery on his girlfriend and tried to stab her. My brotherly senses started tingling. Had to protect my girls."

"She meant it, you know."

The stark awe on his face makes me smile. "I've never had a real family before. It's…" This time it's Eric who's lost for words.

"I know." I hug him a little tighter then straighten as Mary bounces over to us, Wade right beside her.

"Wade, this is my family. Emma and Eric."

"You two twins or something?" Wade's gaze bounces between us, and Eric and I burst out laughing.

Wade lifts an eyebrow questioningly.

"No, they're not." Mary rushes to explain. "You could say the three of us chose each other. We're not related by blood."

"That's cool." His voice wasn't quite deep, but it wasn't high either. "Family's family, no matter how you come to be that way."

That earns him a little more respect.

"Mary said you have your own YouTube show?" Eric releases me and leans against the car, crossing his arms. His blue eyes, usually friendly, seem a little more reserved. It's way more effective than the furrowed brow.

A grin breaks out over Wade's face. "We're the Ghost Chasers online. We go in and investigate rumors of hauntings and things like that. It's why we're here at the Duchaines' today. My cousin told me about what's been happening to them and thought we might be able to help."

I have to wonder if he's ever come in contact with a real ghost. He's too eager. Ghosts are dangerous and scary on the best days, and those are the ones that mean no harm. A ghost that's been here too long after death and gone bad? It's a person's worst nightmare.

"Do you guys just record stuff, or do you do any actual extermination?" Eric asks, bringing my attention back to the conversation.

"We're not Ghostbusters or anything." This from one of the other guys who's carrying a camera with a microphone attached to it. "You can't trap them, but we talk and try to convince them to move on. Stuff like that."

"And does it ever work?" This guy is cute. Black hair cut super short, but left a little longer on the top, glints in the sun as he shades his brown eyes. Eric's noticed how cute he is too, only he tries to hide his reaction. Can't hide it from me, though. I know him too well.

He turns those brown eyes on me with an appreciative look. "Sometimes."

"This is our camera and sound guy, Ethan Cooper. Jordan Hershey," Wade throws his thumb toward the van where Jordan is struggling with some heavy equipment, "is our computer tech." The guy looks scrawny, his curly red hair flapping in the wind.

Eric frowns and pushes off the car to go give him a hand. He's a football player and easily picks up the heavy cases. Jordan says something to him, and Eric nods, heading back our way.

Ethan is watching them, his face closed off, but I don't miss the spark of interest before he shuts it down. Maybe Eric isn't the only one running from feelings. This might be an interesting afternoon after all.

"Everyone ready to go in and meet the family?" Wade gestures toward the house.

"Sure," I agree and follow them inside the very un-haunted house.

The woman who answers the door is in her late twenties with blonde hair cut into a short, fashionable bob. Wary green eyes regard us. Good. I'm hoping at least one person in this house has some sense.

"Mrs. Duchaine?" Wade sticks out his hand. "I'm Wade Poole of Ghost Chasers. Your husband and I spoke on the phone yesterday about opening an investigation here."

Her pink, gloss-covered lips flatten out into a frown. Someone is definitely not happy.

"I did not agree to this."

Wade isn't deterred. "That's okay,

ma'am. I know this probably seems ridiculous, but it's only some questions today. Nothing invasive."

"Who's at the door, Hillary?"

A man with brown hair, holding a little girl of about two or three, comes to the door. His brown eyes take us in all at once. The smile on his face is a stark contrast to his wife's.

"You must be Wade. Come in, come in." He gently pulls his wife away from the doorway, and we pile in. While Wade and the Duchaines chat, I look around. Hardwood floors span the open concept of the main living area. It all looks new inside. Much nicer than the outside, honestly. There's a definite white color scheme running throughout the living room-kitchen combination.

How they manage to keep this place spotless around a toddler is beyond me. The few times my foster homes had little ones in them, the place was always a mess, stains everywhere. This place looks pristine.

"I thought there were only three of

you?" Mr. Duchaine's question garners my full attention.

"They're trainees," Wade replies smoothly.

Eric and I look at each other. Trainees?

It's all we can do to keep a straight face.

Trainees, indeed.

"Oh, I guess that's okay." The man runs a hand through his hair. "Where do you want to do this?"

"Wherever is most comfortable for you." Wade's smile reminds me of a car salesman, and the points he earned earlier dwindle slightly. I hate people who aren't genuine. I'm pretty sure this guy is only after likes for his channel and not into helping this family.

Mary likes him, though, so I'll keep my opinion to myself.

"Let's use the dining room table." Mr. Duchaine gestures toward the big oak table then goes and deposits his daughter behind a baby gate. He turns on some cartoons and checks to make sure there is nothing she could get hurt on.

The baby looks around apprehensively when her father leaves. It's a strange expression for a toddler to wear. The first stirrings of unease tickle my spine. Maybe I'm wrong about this place, but so far nothing has jumped out at me except the little girl's fear.

The guys set up the equipment, and Mary slides up next to me, nodding toward the little girl. "She's afraid."

"I know."

"You see…?"

"You hear…?"

We both stop and shake our heads, neither of us sensing anything supernatural here.

"Girls!" Wade calls, and we reluctantly leave the little girl alone and join them at the dining room table. Jordan's head is bent over his laptop, and Ethan is behind the camera, explaining what he's doing to Eric. I nudge Mary and tilt my head their way. She smiles but doesn't make a fuss about it. Best to let that alone and see where it goes.

Wade is sitting across from Mrs.

Duchaine, who looks about as uncomfortable as a cat in water. He presses record on a digital voice recorder sitting between them. Not sure why he needs it, since Ethan is recording the whole thing, but what do I know?

"This is Ethan Poole at the Duchaine home speaking. The date is August twenty-second, two thousand eighteen. We are entering our first interview session with Henry Duchaine and his wife Hillary. Mr. and Mrs. Duchaine, do you agree you are giving this interview freely and with no coercion on the part of the Ghost Chasers?"

They both give their verbal agreement.

"Can you tell me about the incidents you are experiencing?" Wade opens his notebook and clicks his pen, preparing to take notes.

"I guess it started the night we moved in." Mr. Duchaine frowns, thinking hard. "We started noticing little things at first, nothing major."

"What little things?"

"The lights would flicker, which was

odd. We'd replaced all the wiring and the plumbing when we updated the house. There shouldn't be any issues. Our electrician confirmed he couldn't find anything when he checked it out."

"So, the lights flickering, that happened more than once?"

Mr. Duchaine nods. "All the time, especially in Hailey's room."

"Hailey is your daughter?"

"She's three." Mrs. Duchaine finally speaks up.

"What else did you notice?"

He should have kept on that line of questioning, but I can only hope he goes back to it. Ghosts tend to migrate toward little kids. Their energy is pure and innocent.

"All the sinks in the house like to turn on by themselves. Sometimes it's just a drip, other times, we find the faucet running full force. Plumber agreed with the electrician. There's no reason for it."

Classic signs of a haunting. Anyone can Google it, but I don't think this couple did that. The wife looks upset and uncomfortable. She doesn't want us here or knowing her business.

I glance back over to the makeshift playroom. The baby hasn't left the gate. She's staring at her daddy, her eyes imploring him to come get her. She could simply want out, but there's something about her expression that denies that.

"Interesting." Wade scribbles in his notebook. "Has there been anything else unusual you've noticed?"

"There's a rancid scent that comes and goes. At first, we thought maybe an animal had crawled under the house and died, but the smell didn't stay in any one place. It travels all over the house now."

"Does it seem to linger in any one room longer than the others?"

"In the baby's room." Mrs. Duchaine purses her lips and glances toward the playroom. "Any room she's in, really."

Wade nods and writes a few more things. "Have you seen any apparitions?"

Mrs. Duchaine shakes her head, but her husband nods. Another clue maybe this couple isn't lying to try to get their fifteen minutes of fame on some show. We might be making a second trip here without the Ghostbuster wannabes.

Wade lifts a brow, waiting for them to come to a consensus.

"I saw something," Mr. Duchaine says after a silent moment. "Hillary thinks I'm imagining things, but I don't think so."

"What did you see?"

"I think it was a woman. It had a dress on, anyway. Long, white hair, but I couldn't see the face well. It was white with dark streaks. It's like she'd used black makeup, and it all ran down her face. Mostly, it was just a blur."

"Have you done recent construction?"

The Duchaines are saved from answering by the doorbell. Surprised, Mr. Duchaine glances in that direction.

"Here are my experts." Mrs. Duchaine stands, a relieved expression on her face.

Wait...she doesn't want Wade here, but she called her own ghostbusters? That doesn't make a whole lot of sense.

A familiar voice fills the air, and I turn, not prepared to see who's standing in the doorway, but there he is.

Dr. Lawrence Olivet, spook doctor extraordinaire.

He's always reminded me of Will from *Will and Grace*. It's the brown hair, brown eyes, and shape of his face. He's not overly tall, but not average either. His eyes are always kind, and he has this way of sucking you in when he speaks.

Once upon a time, I considered him family.

Then I found out he'd been lying to me from day one. Once you lose my trust, it's almost impossible to get it back. Thanks to Dan, I didn't completely cut Doc out. I've been trying to rebuild our relationship. Well, trying would be too generous of a word. I haven't ignored his emails or texts. That counts as trying. Maybe.

If he's here, something's definitely up. I hope he can read the warning in my eyes. I'm not here as the Ghost Girl, but as Mary's friend.

Wade's indrawn breath tells me he knows who's just entered the room.

Anyone worth a grain of salt in the paranormal community knows who Doc is. He's always on the move doing lectures, investigating, and recently he's been doing the talk show rounds.

Mr. Duchaine gets up and goes to meet Doc. Wade's eyes nearly bug out of his head. I snicker and try to disguise it as a sneeze, but he's not fooled. He frowns, clearly not appreciating the humor in any of this. Ghostbuster wannabe meets the real deal. *I* can see the humor in it.

Mary stomps on my foot, and Wade doesn't miss the low "ouch" that escapes me. A shy smile flirts with his lips when he looks at Mary. At least I know he's smitten too, and it's not a one-way crush. I'll take a few foot bruises if it means my sister is happy.

Doc follows the Duchaines back into the room, and Wade jumps up like an eager puppy and rushes over to him. It reminds me of my Hellhound, Peaches. She still rushes me like a puppy every time I come home. Peaches was my grandfather Silas's gift to me after I smashed my soul to destroy a Fallen Angel. He wanted to make sure I was always protected and gave me one of his hounds. Oh, and Silas is a demon. Let's not forget that little fact.

Doc smiles and shakes Wade's hand, but his eyes never leave me. He's studying me, making sure I'm okay, I think. It's been a year since we've been in the same room together. Eric squeezes my hand around the same time my phone buzzes.

I know who it is before I look at it. We have a connection forged in our souls, one that time or distance can't break. Sure enough, Dan's texted to see if I'm okay. He must have sensed the trepidation sending butterflies roaming in my stomach. Our connection isn't the same as the one I shared with Eli, my very own Guardian Angel, but it's just as strong, maybe more so since our souls are tied to each other.

A long story in and of itself, and one I don't have time to think about right now. I send him a quick text telling him I'm okay and I'll call him later.

"Emma Rose."

I take a deep breath and bring my eyes back up to meet Doc's. At least he didn't call me Mattie. It sounds strange hearing him call me Emma Rose, though. There are only two people who do that. One is my father, and the other is Silas.

"Hey, Doc."

Wade's eyes go wide when I greet the famous parapsychologist like an old friend. *Ha, take that, Mr. YouTuber*.

"What are you doing here?"

"We're interns, learning the ghost hunting business from Wade, here. He has his own YouTube channel." *Interns* sounds better than trainees.

Doc tilts his head, his gaze bouncing between me, Mary, and Eric. "Well, then, I hope you're learning something."

"Loads." I nod emphatically. I don't want another foot stomp.

"Catch me up on what I missed." Doc settles down across from me, while the Duchaines take their seats. It's hard to miss the stares they're giving me.

While Wade sums up everything from his notes, I check out the baby. She's abandoned her perch at the baby gate and is sitting on her little pink Hello Kitty toddler sofa watching cartoons. She's not nervous, so that's a good thing.

"Hillary, you said you've noticed a lot of activity in the baby's room?" Doc asks, bringing my attention back to the conversation. Finally, someone is focusing on that little tidbit of information.

"Yes, Lawrence. The lights flicker constantly, the TV goes on and off, the baby monitor fritzes out every five minutes. It can get very cold in there too. I'm worried to leave her alone. We've been bringing her into our room at night."

"That's a good thing. A child's energy is the purest there is. Most supernatural beings like ghosts or demons tend to feed off their energy. Has she been irritable or lethargic at all?"

Wade is furiously scribbling during all this. About time he learned some good investigative techniques. Not that his

50

questions were bad, they just didn't dig deep enough.

"She's been fussier than usual." Mr. Duchaine strokes his chin thoughtfully. "Which I thought was the reason she seemed more tired than usual. She's constantly waking up at night."

Doc nods. "We need to secure her safety first. We may have to move her out of the house until this is dealt with. Can she stay with her grandparents if necessary?"

"Of course. Either of our parents would watch her for a few days."

Doc and I both snort at this. He smiles while everyone stares at me like I've just sprouted devil horns. What? I know this isn't going to get sorted quickly. It could take a day, or it could take a couple weeks. It depends on the ghost. Some are easily dealt with, while others are stubborn. And some are just downright evil. The extraction timetable always comes down to that.

"We'll start with a few days and go from there." Doc sits up and leans forward, his arms braced on the dining room table. "Now, you told me over the phone you've done some major renovations. Did all this start happening before or after?"

"We didn't live here before," Mrs. Duchaine explains. "Henry inherited the house from his uncle, who'd been in a specialized facility for Alzheimer's. Even his father didn't know about the house. He was surprised when they read the will. The place has been empty since the early seventies and needed a lot of renovation. There was enough money in the inheritance to make that possible. We moved in a week after everything was done."

"Did the work crews complain about anything unusual?" Doc leans back and takes a sip from the bottle of water he brought in with him.

"Not that they told us." Mr. Duchaine frowns, thinking. "The work got done on time. We started noticing things our first night here, so I don't know how they couldn't have experienced something."

"A lot of times people ignore what's happening around them because they think if they don't acknowledge it, then it's not real. If you can get me the name of the site supervisor, I'll have a chat with him."

"Of course." Mr. Duchaine nods.

The first sliver of unease creeps up on me. It teases the edges of my gifts, testing to see if I feel it. I ignore it, as I am apt to do. Ignore them, and they go away. This time, I want it to think I don't know it's here.

Because something dangerous *is* in this house. It might not feel or look like it at first glance, but it hides in the shadows.

I keep my back to the cold sliver that floats behind me and focus on Doc. He has paused in his questioning and is staring at the spot I ignored. Doc may not be able to see or hear ghosts, but he is sensitive to them. Has been since he was a kid. It's why he works to prove they are real and help those in need.

"How soon can you get your daughter out of the house?"

"Is that really necessary?" Mr. Duchaine asks.

"Henry, Lawrence knows what he's doing. We should listen to him." His wife grips his hand and speaks with urgency.

"How do you know this man?" Mr. Duchaine doesn't look happy.

"Doc is the best in the field." I speak up to keep from turning around. The thing is right there, boring holes into me. A shiver threatens, but I force it back. I have more control than I used to. "Google him."

"How do you know Dr. Olivet?" Wade asks, eyeballing me suspiciously.

"Emma was my intern for an investigation a while back. She's good at this sort of thing."

Wade narrows his eyes before swinging them to Mary. He has to be questioning everything she's told him. What she told him, exactly, I have no idea, but I can feel her starting to shut down. Not gonna happen on my watch.

"I went through a phase." I shrug like it's no big deal. "Mary's more into this stuff than I am."

Wade's expression clears somewhat, but I can still see the questions he's sure to hit us with later rattling around.

"I would like to set up and observe overnight." Doc pulls the conversation back to the pertinent talk of the haunting. "We have to make sure it's an actual haunting instead of the house settling from the renovation."

"Do you really think it could be that simple?" Mrs. Duchaine looks so hopeful, I hate to burst her bubble. Doc must feel the same, because he smiles gently.

"A lot of my investigations end up with me debunking everything. It's rare to find an actual haunting or possession."

"Possession?" Mrs. Duchaine's eyes widen.

"Let's not borrow trouble if we don't have to. I'd like to come back tonight, if possible, with some people to set up a few cameras and microphones in all the hot spots. Ghosts like to come out at night, usually, but not always." Again, his eyes move to the spot behind me where it's still cold.

"Well, Wade had planned on doing that tomorrow night..." Mr. Duchaine trails off at his wife's very hostile snarl.

"I am more than happy to have Wade along," Doc says smoothly, never missing a beat. "That is, if he doesn't mind me tagging along?"

"No, sir." I'm surprised his eyes are still in his head at this point. "It would be an honor to work with you."

"See?" Doc beams at him. "It's all settled."

Mrs. Duchaine does not look happy, but she agrees, and soon we are packing everything up and moving outside. Doc stops by my car while Eric and Mary help Wade's guys load everything back into the van.

"Mat..." He breaks off when I shake my head. No one calls me that anymore except for Dan. He tried, but in the end, he told me I'll always be Mattie Hathaway to him. I let it slide because deep in my soul, I am Mattie Hathaway, no matter how much I try to deny it. Dan is a reminder of that.

"Emma." He corrects himself and smiles ruefully. "How are you doing? Everything okay with your father?"

Doc doesn't trust my dad as far as he can throw him. Granted, my dad is pretty scary to everyone but me. He has criminal tendencies, but so do I. He even admitted to me he planned on sacrificing me to gain my abilities. It's what the Oracle he consulted told him he had to do to gain the power he wanted, but once he held me, that idea went out the window. My dad loves me. He'd never harm me in any way, shape, or form. It's an undeniable truth I feel every time I'm near Zeke.

"Things are great, Doc. You don't have to worry about me."

The frown he's sporting clearly says he thinks he does. I don't really care what he thinks about Zeke. I know the truth, and that's all that counts.

Instead of arguing, he steers the conversation back to the house. "Intern?"

"Mary's into Wade, but she didn't want to come by herself around a bunch of guys she'd never met. Eric and I tagged along. Wade explained the extra bodies by calling us trainees."

"That was smart," Doc agrees. "Will the three of you be coming back tonight?"

"I don't know. We were only here to support Mary. We're not really part of the fake ghostbusters team."

Doc gestures toward the house. "What do you think?"

"At first, I didn't think this place was haunted."

"It doesn't look like the normal haunting grounds." Doc leans against my car. "But when Hillary called, I agreed to come. Her mother and I are friends."

Well, that explains how she got the famous spook doctor here. "Just friends?"

He blushes, and I grin. Doc has a girlfriend.

"We're taking it slow."

"Uh-huh."

Doc is quick to change the subject.

"Did you sense anything in there?"

That wipes the smile off my face. "Yeah, and nothing good either. That thing is angry."

"Am I right to worry about the baby?"

"Yeah, I think you are. Not sure she should stay there even one more night."

"Will you come back tonight and help me? You have an advantage I think we'll need, especially in the baby's room."

"I don't know…" My gaze goes over to the fake ghostbusters. I don't want them to know what I can do and have it all over YouTube. I came to New Orleans to escape all that.

"They don't need to know about your abilities. We can keep that between you and me."

"They're going to set up cameras, Doc. I don't think me confronting a ghost is going to escape their attention."

The van pulls away from the curb, and Mary and Eric join us, ready to go.

"How about you and I walk the house now while there are no cameras?" Doc suggests.

I want to say no. Really, I do, but the image of the toddler's eyes begging her Daddy to rescue her haunts me.

"Did you feel that in there?" Mary shivers, looking at the house.

"I'm not a ghost anymore, but even I felt that. The cold felt almost angry, like it wanted us gone." Eric's gaze is fixated on the front window, where the curtains are moving gently as if by a breeze. Could be the air from an AC vent, but I don't think so. That thing is watching us, calculating our next move.

It's smart.

But I'm a reaper.

"Let's go back inside and see what we're dealing with."

The Duchaines are surprised when Doc knocks on the door with Wade's interns.

"Hillary, I wanted to talk to you without the cameras." Doc sits on the couch when we're all back inside. "I want to protect Ma…Emma's privacy."

"Privacy?" Mr. Duchaine gives me a curious stare.

"Yes," I say and glance toward the baby's playroom. "Can you get your daughter? I'd feel more comfortable if she was safe before we start. In fact, I think it might be better if she's not in the house at all while we walk it."

"There's something here, isn't there?"

Mrs. Duchaine asks while her husband collects the toddler.

I nod, sweeping the room. Ghosts are tricky beasts. They can hide, even from me, for a short while. "At first, I didn't think so. This place is just too normal. Ghosts typically hang out in old abandoned places or homes that are rundown a bit. You don't find them often in homes like this."

"Who are you, exactly?" Mr. Duchaine sits back down, the baby in his arms. She's smiling. It's the first smile I've seen on her face all day.

"My name is Emma Crane, and for lack of a better description, I see ghosts."

"Crane..." Mr. Duchaine frowns. "Are you related to Ezekiel Crane?"

"He's my dad."

A flash of unease creeps into his eyes. "Your father..." He breaks off, and I decide to put him at ease.

"He's not a good person, I know, but when it comes to me, he's my dad, and he loves me. Me walking your house has nothing to do with him, but with me wanting to protect your daughter. This thing is feeding off her. A child's essence or soul, or whatever you want to call it, is the purest form of energy imaginable. If we don't stop this thing, it will drain her dry, and she'll die."

He still looks uneasy. My dad has a reputation in this town, a reputation that most don't want anything to do with. I can understand Mr. Duchaine's hesitation.

"Henry, even if you don't trust the Crane name, trust *me*. This girl is nothing like her father. She can help you if you let her. All we're asking is to walk the house. Will you at least let us do that?"

"Does the other ghost team know about this?" Mr. Duchaine asks.

"They don't know what I can do, and I'd like to keep it that way. I have no desire to be on a YouTube show. I wasn't even supposed to be here today, but I got roped into it. I'm going to count that as a sign that maybe I was led here." I look pointedly at their little girl.

"It's just a walk-through, Henry." Mrs.

Duchaine squeezes his hand. "If they can help, we should let them."

"You didn't even believe anything was wrong."

"No, Henry, I knew something wasn't right, but in my family, you don't share this kind of thing with outsiders. I didn't want the cameras here, but I gave in because of Hailey. I want her safe."

His arms tighten around the little girl. "That's all I want too."

"Then let Lawrence and Emma walk the house and maybe find out what we're dealing with."

His lips brush the top of his daughter's head. That one is definitely going to be a daddy's girl. "Okay."

"Can you take the baby out of the house for a little while? I don't want her here while we do this." I glance around, searching for our mystery ghost, but it isn't anywhere to be seen. Not surprised. Ghosts can't hide from me long, though. They can't resist my own light, as Zeke tells me. I'm like a beacon in a raging storm.

"Sure. We can take her to the park. She loves it." Mrs. Duchaine stands and nudges her husband to get moving.

While he doesn't look happy, he does as he is asked, and we are all alone in the house with something that doesn't want to be found and doesn't want to leave its food source.

"How you want to do this, Hathaway?" Eric's gaze searches the room. He's never really said if any of his residual ghost abilities are still there, and I never pressed him. He has enough going on learning to live in someone else's skin and getting adjusted to having parents again.

"It's better if I do this alone." Not that I want to do this alone, but I'd put both Mary and Eric in danger more than once. Well, Eric's body. Jake got shot because of me. I lost so much that day. Those memories will haunt me until the day I die.

Nope, not going there. Getting inside my head won't help me right now.

"Not a chance, Hathaway." Eric's eyes

turn steely. "You get into too much trouble on your own."

"Why don't we compromise?" Doc suggests. "You go first, and we'll follow. Once you clear a room, we'll go in, record it, and take some photos. That way you're not more than a few feet away from us, and you stay off camera."

"You're recording?"

"Of course." Doc nods like I should know this. "I want to document the haunting. Sometimes my specialized equipment picks up things the human eye can't see, or that we can't hear, for that matter." I raise an eyebrow, and he chuckles. "Well, that most of us can't hear."

"Give me five minutes by myself before you come in." Ghosts don't like groups. It's a known fact. They tend to stray toward the loner, that person getting up in the middle of the night to go to the bathroom or get a drink of water. They're like predators in that way, singling out the solitary member of the herd.

"That's fine. I need to get some

equipment out of the car. We'll go outside while you do a short walkthrough first. Eric can wait right by the front door in case you need help."

Eric still wants to argue, but he agrees. I want him and Mary both out of the house for the entire thing, but that isn't happening either.

Once everyone is outside, I take a deep breath. It's been a while since I actually went looking for a ghost that was hiding. Thanks to the spelled tattoos I have on my body, they can't overwhelm me anymore or make me feel their deaths, but they can still terrify me. Some of them died some pretty gruesome deaths, and that is how they appear to me. I see every injury on their bodies. And the ones that have gone bad? Even worse.

Well, here goes nothing.

Opening up that part of myself that is a reaper sorta feels like I'm a pebble skipping over the water, feeling the surface ripple beneath me as waves spread out from the simple movement I've caused. My gift is a lake that lives inside me, and I'm the pebble skipping over it, but today, I want to feel all of it, not just the ripples. So instead of skipping like I normally do, I let myself sink inside the icy cold waters until I'm at the very heart of it, drowning in the cold.

Drowning terrifies me because a very angry ghost did drown me last year. If it hadn't been for Eli giving me CPR, I would have died.

I used to fight this feeling, but Zeke taught me better. He knows about my newfound fear of drowning and how hard it is to let this in, but he was right. When I stopped panicking and fighting the sensation, it became easier and didn't last as long.

The cold seeps into me, chasing away the heat until every cell in my body is nothing but the icy cold of the reaper. She's death, and there is no warmth for the dead.

The water swirls around me, gently pushing me back to the surface, and when I open my eyes, I know without looking in a mirror my eyes are glowing the color of a cold February sky instead of the hazel they normally are. Remnants of my mother's abilities. She bound most everything I can do except for my reaping abilities. The glow of my eyes is the one piece of her that remains.

Time to hunt.

Keeping my arms by my side, I extend my fingertips and imagine tendrils of my magic escaping, forming long cords of smoke and mist as it fans out, searching for the ghost hiding in this house.

Echoes of screams and cries rise up to hound me, but I push them back. Those creatures reside outside this house, and they're not the one I'm looking for.

"It's going to do you no good to hide. I will find you." I don't raise my voice, but I know the ghost can hear me.

The kitchen is right off the living room. I'm guessing they tore down a few walls in here. All the walls look new. The kitchen is a black and white affair, white cabinets, black countertops, with a black and white subway tile backsplash. Very modern. The sink is dripping. There's a very faint signature here, like the ghost idly turned it on in passing. I turn it off and continue down the hall off the kitchen. There's a powder room and an office back here. Neither room holds my interest.

The door to the basement is in the kitchen, but I'll go downstairs with Doc and the others. Dark basements are like the morgue. You don't do them by yourself. Bad things live in the dark.

I begin walking toward the hallway off the living room, letting my gifts scout ahead.

Nothing.

With each step I take, it gets noticeably colder. I don't hear the AC running.

The first room I come to is the master bedroom. Walking in, I halt in the middle of the room and close my eyes. There was something here. Maybe just minutes ago. The energy here, while not strong, is definitely the same thing I felt behind me earlier. It's spent time in here. The Duchaines have been bringing Hailey to bed with them, and this thing searches her out in here.

I check the bathroom then head down the hall until I come to the baby's room. The door has her name spelled out in colorful letters. The room itself is done in hues of pink and summer green. A few gray splashes here and there. The crib is white, as well as all the other furniture in the room. A toybox made to look like a castle sits in one corner, and a rocking chair is to the right of the crib. A carousel adorns the night stand by the crib.

A perfectly adorable room for a perfectly adorable little girl.

None of this stands out, but it's at least ten degrees cooler in this room than it is out in the hallway. I put my hands on the crib, close my eyes, and concentrate.

At first, I see nothing, but then images start to flash in front of me until I'm spinning away into a memory.

The baby's asleep, the carousel playing a lullaby, and the soft lights splash images of dancing fairies across the walls and the ceiling.

Mrs. Duchaine leans down and strokes the child's cheek, tucking a blanket around her before leaving and closing the door.

The room darkens, and a cold so icy that it steals my breath enters. My teeth rattle, I'm shaking so hard. I've never felt such a bitter cold, and I've been in some terrifying places. This, though? It's a black void of nothingness that's always hungry, always searching for a way to make the hunger ease.

She floats up through the floor directly beneath the rocking chair. It's definitely a woman. Her hair is as white as the snow that used to fall in Charlotte. Her dark blue dress is old, and I can't quite place the fashion to know the era she's from. Black streaks coat her face, just like Mr. Duchaine described. Her eyes are pitch black when she looks at me. The pallor of her face doesn't look like that of the dead, but instead like she's wearing costume makeup, like a clown or mime. The black circles around her eyes and the black of her lipstick stand out against all that white. That's where the black streaks are coming from.

The hatred surrounding her is intense. She makes a beeline for the crib, and as a result, lands smack dab in the middle of me because of where I'm standing. I keep my hands pressed tight to the crib, ignoring the urge to run screaming from the room. This is a memory. Not the ghost herself. No matter how many times I tell myself that, it doesn't make it any easier to stand here.

She reaches down and runs a finger along the baby's cheek, drawing a wisp of smoke from her. Leaning down, she gets close to the little girl's face and inhales deeply. More wispy lines of smoke float up from the baby and into the ghost. Hailey whimpers in her sleep as the thing feeds from her.

The blanket gets thrown off as the toddler stirs, kicking out and turning over on her side. The ghost's rage deepens, and she puts her hands on the child and rolls her over. She inhales again, and a sucking sound emerges from her, like's she's latched onto Hailey's flesh and is pulling the life out of her.

The baby wakes and looks up into the cold, obsidian eyes of the monster and starts screaming for all she's worth. A dry cackle leaves the entity. It's laughing, enjoying the fear and the pain.

It doesn't take long for her father to burst into the room and pick her up, severing the tie to the ghost.

And that enrages the ghost.

Books fly off the shelf, and toys are thrown across the room. The carousel smashes to the floor, and the thing stalks toward Mr. Duchaine, only he doesn't wait around. He runs out of the room.

She snarls but can't seem to go after them, which only makes her madder. She trashes the room, and her silent scream echoes around me, filtering through my head like a sharp knife slicing as it goes. Each wail is a nail driven through my eardrums.

Hands grip my shoulders and shake me.

She looks directly at me.

No, this is a memory. She can't see me.

Her head is tilted down, her chin almost resting on her chest. Her eyes look up, the angle making her appear even more hostile. She is nothing but pain and rage. It burns and sparks in her like embers, catching flame and spreading like wildfire, destroying everything in its path.

The hands gripping me shake me harder, but I'm caught. I can't look away from her.

She smiles.

I shudder away from her and that smile.

"Mattie!"

I jerk at the sound of my name, blinking.

She puts a finger to her lips then sinks back down in the floor.

"This is why I didn't want her going in by herself. I swear to God…"

My knees buckle, and I would have fallen if not for Eric holding me. Reality sweeps back in, and I lean against him, desperate for warmth.

I'm shaking, I'm so cold.

Did that thing feed off me?

My phone goes off about the same time my head rolls to the side and the dark rushes in to claim me.

Whispers everywhere.

Shadows rippling over every surface.

My head is killing me, and I'm cold, but I can't seem to wake up. I need to get up and turn the heat on. Mary forgets to do it sometimes, especially when she's hot.

"Be still, my darling girl. You're going to injure yourself."

I know that voice all too well.

Silas.

"I…" My throat aches.

"What did I just tell you?" He sounds cranky, which isn't a good thing for me. He tends to do me serious harm when

77

he's cranky. Grandfather or not, Silas is still a demon who does what needs to be done, no matter who gets hurt in the process. Including me.

After everything I've seen and done, nothing truly frightens me anymore. Granted, ghosts can still get the jump on me and scare me for a minute, because who really expects to turn around and see a dead person staring at you? But that fear goes away.

The exception to the rule is Silas.

He's never once lied to me, and he's flayed the skin from my face, something I will never forget. Sometimes I can still feel the pain and will grip my cheek when the memory haunts me. Silas doesn't make threats, he only speaks in truths. When he says he'll hurt you, he will.

I'm probably the only person he regrets ever having to hurt, but that doesn't mean he won't do it again if he thinks it's necessary.

Something cold and wet rubs across the back of my leg. The distinct stench of rubbing alcohol tickles my nose.

"What are you doing?"

He stops, and a loud sigh echoes through the room. "Can you never listen? The more you question me, the longer this will take."

"If you'll tell me what *this* is, I might stop asking questions."

"It's me preventing you from being a tasty snack for the monsters. Now, don't move. It's going to hurt."

With that, he set in with his needle. More tattoos.

And boy, did it hurt. I've noticed some of the tattoos he's given me over the years hurt more than others. Like the full body one on my back. It runs from my neck all the way down to the soles of my feet. It was designed to help me against the Fallen Angel, Deleriel. I survived it, but Eli didn't, and that's something that will haunt me until I die.

Silas works on the back of my left calf as I clench my teeth. He never uses any kind of numbing agent, saying it interferes with the magical properties of the ink. While I appreciate that fact, I'd rather be knocked out during the process. Sometimes I do sleep through the smaller ones, but when I wake up, he never puts me back to sleep.

"Isn't that going to interfere with the one already back there?" I need to talk to distract myself from the pain.

"Emma Rose." The finality in his voice makes me tense. He's getting angry—not irritated, but angry. "If you keep talking, I will be forced to sew your mouth shut until I am done, and trust me when I tell you, the needle flowing through your lips will hurt far more than this tattoo needle."

I let out a frustrated sigh. He'll do it. I know he will.

"And no, it's not going to interfere with your protection sigil. I'm weaving this design through that one. It's why I need to concentrate. One small slip, and both are ruined."

He goes back to inking, and I grit my teeth. Pain and I do not get along. Any kind of pain. I've been put through so much of it over the course of my life, I should be used to it by now, but who really gets used to pain? No one I've ever met.

I can sense her before I see her. Peaches. My own personal Hellhound. Silas gave her to me after the whole mess with Deleriel. He keeps her here while I'm at college. Can't very well have a Hellhound haunting the halls of Tulane.

Peaches was the runt of the litter, but you wouldn't know that now. As she comes into what little light there is, my eyes widen. She's grown at least a foot taller and maybe three feet wider than when last I saw her. Her fur is the same soft chocolate color it was when she was just a puppy. Her eyes are red, but that is to be expected. She's a beast of Hell. I don't hold it against her.

She licks my face, and I scrunch up my nose. Dog slobber. Peaches knows I hate doggie slobber, and she does it to irritate me, I think. Not that I'd ever fuss at her, but still. Just *ewww*!

"Down, girl." Silas's strict tone makes

me cringe, but the dog ignores him. She rubs her face against mine and whines, wanting some loving.

"She hasn't seen me in a week, Silas." I keep my tone even so as not to set him off. "She just wants some attention."

"She can have attention later when you're not in danger of losing every ounce of protection I've been able to provide for you."

He's gone from testy to angry. "Go on, girl. I'll come see you in a while."

Peaches gives me one last whine and trots off the way she came. I hear the huff and grin. Peaches doesn't listen to Silas when I'm around, and it frustrates him. He did transfer ownership of her to me, so he shouldn't be shocked. A Hellhound obeys its owner, not its breeder.

The next hour is a slow and painful one, full of silence aside from the sound of the tattoo needle. Just when I think I can't take any more, he stops. Thank God. I might have done something stupid soon and ended up with my lips sewn together.

"There." Silas puts down his instruments and applies a bandage to my leg. "Don't let this get wet for a few days."

"I know the routine." I blink and gingerly sit up, finally getting a look around. We're not in his usual studio. It looks more like a cave, with rock walls and a hard-packed dirt floor. "Where are we?"

"In my basement." He washes his hand in a bowl sitting on an old-fashioned table that could have been a hundred years old or made yesterday. It's hard to tell in the dim lighting.

"Why?"

"Because there are protection sigils down here that aren't in the main house." He doesn't explain further and motions for me to follow him to the steep set of stairs nestled against one rock wall.

"Why do we need protection sigils?"

"Why do you always ask so many questions?" he grumbles irritably.

"Because I do." Peaches falls into step beside me, and I scratch her ear as we walk. "When you decide to go all cloak and dagger, it makes me insanely curious. Plus, if there's some kind of danger, I'd rather know about it first and be prepared."

His fists clench, and I'm afraid I've pushed him too far. He is crankier than usual today.

"Do you think Deleriel is the only Fallen Angel on the Earth, Emma Rose?"

The words are said so softly, I'd have missed them if I hadn't been right beside him. More Fallen Angels? My hands start to shake. I'd only ever faced one, and defeating him had shattered my soul. I don't think I can do that again.

"I Angel-proofed the basement." Silas opens the door at the top of the stairs. "Even if they wanted to spy on us, they couldn't. In the main house, I have certain sigils up, but not the ones to keep all Angels out."

"So, are they all after me now or something?" My own voice is as quiet and serious as Silas's.

"I don't know."

84

I follow him into his studio, the one I'm familiar with. There is no body on his sterile table today. A canvas sits on the easel waiting to be seen to, but his paints aren't out. I get my own artistic skills from both my mother, Georgina Dubois, and from Silas.

This place has bad memories for me. Silas forced me to learn to use my abilities by experimenting on souls. My blood can pull the soul out of a person and trap it in a canvas, where they'll feel the pain and torture of Hell for an eternity. My mind shudders away from the pain I'd caused, telling me it was necessary to defeat Deleriel and get my sister back.

"Sit." Silas waves to the breakfast table I'm fairly certain wasn't in here a few seconds ago. "You need to eat and regain your strength."

"I'm fine." Peaches doesn't seem to think so, because she pushes me toward the table. "You just want to eat too." I rub her ear affectionately but sit down as she clearly wants me to.

"No, she can sense what I do. Energy has been siphoned off your soul. It's not nearly healed enough to withstand much of that. That boy should never have left until you were healed."

I roll my eyes. Not this again. He'd been furious when Dan went back to North Carolina, but he has a life there. He's got school, work, and his mom's upcoming trial. He had to go back.

"I'm fine, Silas. Really. Dan was here until I stopped hurting every time he was away from me."

When my soul was first put back together, it had been extremely fragile. Dan's soul held mine together, and when he was too far away from me in the beginning, I'd felt a physical pain so severe, I almost went into shock. It had taken months for me to heal enough so he could go home and get back to his own life.

"It is not fine, Mattie Louise Hathaway."

Oh, crap. He only ever calls me that when he is good and truly pissed. I don't even have time to jump up and run before he's all up in my face.

"You think you're fine, do you?" he snarls.

"I don't ache anymore, Silas, not like I did," I whisper, afraid to move, afraid of what he'll do.

He shakes his head then plunges his hand right into my chest. It goes through me like my skin and bones are nothing but smoke and mirrors.

The pain hits as soon as my brain registers what is happening. I open my mouth to scream as his fingers dig around, but no sound comes out. He grabs something inside and starts to withdraw his hand, and the pain intensifies until there is nothing but blinding, searing agony.

When he pulls his hand free, the pain stops, but that isn't all. Something isn't right. I'm not afraid anymore, or even angry. I feel nothing. And I don't care that I feel nothing.

"What did you do?" I cock my head sideways then frown when Peaches growls at me.

Silas unfolds his clenched fist, and there in the center of it lays a tiny ball of bluish-white light.

"Look closely, my darling girl. Look at how much your soul hasn't healed."

I do as he asks, not because I'm curious or even care, but it's something to do. The orb has thousands of tiny cracks and fissures, the light bleeding out of them like blood oozing from a wound. He's correct in that it doesn't look fit to be called a soul. It's demolished. How that thing is even still pulsing is beyond me.

"It's broken."

"Aye." Silas cradles it in his hand like it's something precious, but I've seen him do the same with a thousand souls. I've done it myself. "This is why you can't let your soul be fed upon. It will only take minutes for you and Daniel to die."

I think about that, but again, I feel nothing. What is one more death in the world? People live, and they die. It is the natural order. If I die, then I die. Dan would simply be a casualty of my death.

"I wonder if I shouldn't hold onto this until it's healed enough not to fracture." Silas stares at me, his question clear.

"Do what you want." I shrug. It means nothing to me.

"Your eyes are glowing black." This brings a smile to his face. It makes him happy that my demon side is shining through. With no human soul to police those abilities, I'm not surprised they've decided to make an appearance.

"Your father will never leave me alone if I don't put this back." Silas frowns, his British accent thick as he thinks through his dilemma. It's true enough. My father would torment him if he thought Silas had done something to me.

Sighing heavily, Silas plunges his hand back into my chest, and this time I do scream. I may not feel emotions, but pain, I definitely do. It's a physical reaction, not a metaphysical one. His fingers twist until I hear a popping noise, like a lock clicking into place, and all those emotions that had fled come rushing back.

I hunch over when his hand leaves me, trying to breathe through the pain. His words and my thoughts play back in my head like a recording, and I'm appalled and horrified at my reactions. Let Dan die? Never. Just the thought causes a small panic attack, and my lungs close up.

"Breathe, girl." Silas slaps my back like he would if I were choking. "Just breathe."

"Don't ever do that again." I look up, and he retreats from me. I don't know what he sees in my expression, but for once, it's scared him. I've only ever seen him afraid of me once before, and that was when Dan almost died because of him. Silas may have engineered my birth to get the perfect trifecta of power, but he also knows I can end him.

Not sure how, but it's something I know on a cellular level.

Doesn't mean I'm not terrified of him, or that he can't hurt me.

Him yanking my soul out of me is a case in point.

It just means he knows I have the ability to hurt him if he ever truly makes me angry enough.

The only thing that could cause me to be that angry?

Dan Richards dying.

Never happen.

Not as long as I am alive.

"It was the only way to make you see how precarious your situation is. Letting that soul eater anywhere near you is reckless. You can't go back to that house."

I can see the little girl's terrified expression in my mind's eye. She'll die if I don't help her.

Not gonna happen either.

"I have to go back, Silas." I lean back in the chair, suddenly exhausted. "No one else can. Besides, didn't you just put some kind of tattoo on me to keep that thing from munching on me?"

I rub my chest absently. I don't feel right. I know he put my soul back, but something's off, like a puzzle piece that doesn't fit.

"It'll take a few days to settle back into place." Silas comes closer, seeing most of my anger has dissipated. "It's normal for you to feel odd."

Peaches pushes her face into my stomach and whines. She seems as upset as I am. "Didn't like the soulless me, huh, girl?"

"She's trained to hunt souls and drag them back to Hell." Silas walks over to one of the long cabinets lining the left side of the room and retrieves a tray. "A soulless creature still alive upsets the balance. Peaches wanted to rip your throat out, but her loyalty to you stopped her."

"Good girl." I lean down and hug her. "You know I love you."

Silas sets the tray down to reveal a grilled cheese sandwich, tomato soup, and an icy cold Coke. My favorite. "Now, eat. You need strength."

He fusses until I pick up the sandwich and start to eat. "What do you know about that thing that fed off me?"

"Not any more than what it is. It feeds off souls to stay strong. It can harm you in ways you can't even imagine."

"Care to elaborate on that?"

"No."

He's probably mad I refused to stay away from the danged thing. Oh, well. I eat in silence, slipping Peaches bites of the sandwich when Mr. Grumpy Pants isn't looking.

"How long have I been here?"

"Most of the day." He walks over to the door that's partially hidden behind the wall, and my stomach clenches. His room of lost souls. "Care to help me?"

"No, Silas. I won't do that ever again."

The smile he gives me says how wrong I am. I swore never to do anyone harm, and yet I did to save my sister. Who knows what might make me do that again. He's right. Someday I might be forced to hurt those souls again, but not today.

"If you're going to torture them, I think I'm ready to go." I stand and give my

Hellhound one last hug. "I wanted to show you some new sketches I did. Can I bring them by in a few days?"

"You are welcome here anytime, my darling girl." Silas flashes me a smile and turns back to his room of horrors. "You know the way out."

Yes, I do.

I focus on drawing a doorway and then on the last thing I remember, being in that room, that ghost feeding on me, but I focus on the sound of Mary's and Eric's shouts, their fear for me. Then I walk through the door, right into the moment Silas snatched me away from that reality.

Going from one plane of existence to another isn't exactly painful, but it's *very* disconcerting. It's like in *Star Trek*, where they beam you up, and it forces all your molecules and atoms to disperse then reassemble at your destination. When I'm out there floating, all the pieces of me reaching out, desperate and terrified, I think of it as pain, even though it's not. And when all my bits finally snap back into place, it doesn't stop those first few minutes of panic. My body knows what happened to it, and it needs time to digest that it's whole again.

I can usually handle this because I'm

expecting it, but after Silas's stunt of yanking my soul out of my body, my psyche knows it's not all right.

That's probably why the voices around me are so muddled, and I'm a little dizzy. My vision is blurry, and my head…let's not talk about the massive migraine forming.

I'm not sure how long I lie there, but soon the mumbling becomes clearer.

"…hospital!"

"Just give her a minute."

That voice, I recognize. It's Mary.

"Dan says last time this happened, it almost killed her. He says he's going to fly down here himself if we don't get her to the ER!"

And there's Eric, the worrywart.

There is no way I'm going to a hospital, though. When I open my eyes again, the room is less blurry than before, and the walls have also decided to stay put. I'm good.

Mostly.

"Will you two stop arguing?" I groan and throw an arm over my eyes. My head is soon going to explode.

"Dan? She's awake and as grouchy as a bear."

I am *not* grouchy. I just don't appreciate all the yelling. I hold my free hand out for the phone, knowing Dan really will hop a plane if he thinks I need him.

When the cool metal meets my fingertips, I grasp it and pull it to my ear. "I'm fine. Really."

"Liar." The sound of his voice helps to soothe me more than anything else. "You forget what happens to you happens to me."

"You okay?"

"Aside from feeling like something rammed a fist through my chest, I'm fine." He doesn't even try to hide the sarcasm.

"I'm sorry. I'll see if I can't find something that minimizes your exposure."

"No, you won't." He pauses to answer someone in the background.

"Where are you?"

"I'm at work." He lets out a sigh. "Listen, Squirt, if you do that, then I won't know when you're in trouble."

"The whole point of me coming to New Orleans was to learn to handle things on my own, Officer Dan."

"I know that, Mattie, but I need to know you're okay too."

Dan tried calling me Emma Rose in the beginning, but he gave up after a few days. I'll always be Mattie Hathaway to him.

"Okay, I won't do that if you stop trying to harass Eric into rushing me to the hospital."

"That headache…"

"Will be fine. I'll take the migraine meds they gave me. It's all good. I promise."

"I got to get back to work, but call me later, okay? We'll Skype."

"Sure thing, Officer Dan. Love you."

"Love you too, Squirt."

I listen for him to hang up for a minute and realize he's still on the line. He's waiting for me.

"You gonna hang up or what?"

"When you do."

Shaking my head, I lift my arm enough to be able to see the phone so I can disconnect the call. He'll hold all day if he has to, and I don't want to get him into trouble.

"She's awake?" Doc asks, and I sit up carefully. I don't want the walls to go dark side on me again and start spinning out of control. Despite what I said, I really don't feel so well. Instead of focusing on that, I take stock of the situation.

I'm on the floor, sitting on a white rug with little pink hearts all over it. The room is toasty warm, and there's no sign of the soul eater, as Silas called it. That's a super huge plus right there.

"How do you feel?" Doc kneels in front of me, his hand at his side, but twitchy. He and I are just getting back to being friends. I can see the need to touch me to make sure I'm okay in his expression, but he controls himself. Brownie points to the doc.

"Not so hot. That thing fed on me." Food, then sleep. That's what I need more than anything else.

"That's what I was afraid of," Doc says. "Given everything the family described, it sounds like a type of succubus."

"No, Doc." I accept his offer of help to stand up. "It's something different. It's focused on the kid, not the adults. Succubi tend to feed off sexual energy."

"You've been studying up on your lore." Doc grins, sounding as proud as a papa.

"Well, after everything that happened, I want to be prepared. No one is getting the jump on me ever again. Be it your random run-of-the-mill ghost or some freaking Fallen Angel."

"Fallen Angel?" Mary's voice drops an octave, and I hear the tremor in it. Just the mention of that particular breed of creature sends her spiraling down the rabbit hole. We're just getting her back to her old self. I'm not going to be responsible for her falling into the dark place she goes whenever she thinks of Deleriel.

"Sorry, Mary. It was just a reference, that's all." I make a mental note to ask Silas if he can add the same tattoo to her that he did to me. She deserves to be protected as much as I do.

She lets out a slow breath, and I'm glad I didn't blurt out anything Silas told me. Once we get her inked, I'll tell her everything.

"Do we need to get you checked out at the ER?" Doc asks, concerned. He's probably worried because I'm still holding onto him. I let his hand go and take a few cautious steps toward Mary. When the walls stay put, I know I'm okay.

"No, I'm fine. Really."

Doc quirks a brow at me but doesn't push the subject. "Well, do you think you're still up for playing intern for the next few days?"

"I want that thing away from the baby. It's going to kill her." The reaper in me rebels at the thought of letting that thing loose upon others. It needs to move on, be it to a better place or to somewhere less friendly like The Between, the nothingness between this plane and the next, where there are some very bad things ready to snack on you.

"Then we need to do some research. Find out the history of the home, if there were any deaths here or associated with the property." Doc frowns, thinking. "Those boys will be back tonight, and I'm not sure it's safe for them alone in the house. Perhaps we should come back as well."

"I don't think Mattie's up to facing that thing again," Eric worries.

"I can stay outside in the Scooby van." Mary gives me a disapproving look, which I promptly ignore.

"You can stay in my investigative van. It's equipped with the proper ghost hunting paraphernalia and computers to monitor the feed inside the house."

"Do you have it warded?" I ask, not sure he's up on his demonic and angelic sigils.

"After the…" Doc slides a quick glance at Mary and clears his throat. "After last year, I did my research. That van is impenetrable against most anything, including ghosts. It's our safe zone."

Doc has his stuff straight. I'm impressed. Maybe the wannabes will actually learn something from him.

"I'm not up to hitting the books or looking at a computer screen right now." My head vibrates with anger at the thought. "So, maybe…"

Doc interrupts me. "I'll have Seth do all that. He's my new assistant. Wants to learn the ins and outs of the ghost hunting business."

"When did you get an assistant?" I blink when a sharp stab of pain straight through my temple blindsides me. Dang, but that smarts. I haven't had a headache this bad since I was in the hospital last year.

"About a month ago. Seth has proven quite valuable when it comes to research, and the boy knows how to do what I tell him without asking all kinds of questions. He knows I'll explain everything at some point."

"Cool." One less thing for me to worry about. "Let's get home so I can have a nap. What time should we be back here, Doc?"

"Say around seven? Seth will be here earlier to set up our own cameras. I want my feed separate from those other people."

"The Scooby crew?" I snicker and ignore Mary's ire.

Doc's lips tilt ever so slightly. He's trying not to hurt Mary's feelings, but he and I both know those guys are so far from real ghost hunters, it's not even funny.

"It's a plan. Now, let's get out of here."

No one disagrees with that.

We drop Eric off at his dorm, and then Mary lets me out at ours. She is going to meet up with Wade to catch some dinner before the ghost hunt, so I told her to use my car. No point in her having to park mine then go find hers. She promised to pick me and Eric up by six so we could make it back out to the Duchaines'. Those poor people. They have no idea what is in their house.

I don't either. I'm not quite sure what it is, except that it eats souls. Maybe Doc's assistant will find something. I can only hope so. All the research I've done tells me the more you know about your

105

target, the easier it will be to either get them to move on or to dispose of them for good.

"You sure you'll be okay by yourself?" Mary pulls up to the front of our dorm, worried.

"I'm fine. I just need a power nap, and I'll be good as new."

"You'll call if you get sick?"

"Sure will." I open the car door and get out before she can worry herself into changing her mind about going to meet up with Wade. She deserves a little happiness.

Waving, I head up the stairs of the dorm's front porch, hearing her pull away. I love my sister, but sometimes I need peace and quiet, especially when my head feels like it might implode.

I don't notice him at first. It's not until he stands up from one of the benches along the right side of the porch that I see him. He's tall, well over six feet. Dark brown hair frames hazel eyes. He's staring at me, his eyes curious.

"Hello," he says. His voice is deeper

than I'd expect from someone who looks to be in his early twenties.

"Hey. Do you need some help?" He keeps staring at me, and it's making me nervous.

"Are you Emma Crane?"

All the warning bells and whistles start to go off. Who is he, and how does he know my name?

"Who are you?"

"I'm Aleric Nathaniel Buchard, your brother."

I back away slowly, trying not to panic. Zeke and my grandparents had warned me about the Dubois family. They are way worse than the Cranes, and my grandfather worries they might try to kill me for my gifts.

"Don't be afraid." His hazel eyes, *my eyes*, beseech me to believe him.

"I'm not afraid," I say. "I'm just giving myself room to move in case I need to defend myself."

He grins, a dimple appearing in his cheek. "You're feisty and quick on your feet."

"How did you find out about me?"

"Our mother."

Holy crap. She must have gone back to her parents after she fled the hospital. Of course she'd tell them about me.

I take two more steps backward. Georgina wants me dead.

"I swear I'm not here to hurt you." He comes to stand at the end of the porch. "I just wanted to meet my sister."

He doesn't seem threatening, but I've learned the hard way that doesn't mean jack.

"Will you come sit down for a few minutes so we can talk? We'll stay right here in the open where everyone can see us."

Instead of doing that, I pull out my phone and call Dan. He picks up on the third ring.

"You okay?"

"I'm not sure."

"What's wrong?"

"My brother just showed up at my dorm."

He lets out a string of curses I've never

heard him use. He hates swear words, but boy, is he using them now.

"I'm calling you back on FaceTime." He hangs up, and within a few seconds, he's back. His brown eyes are intense, full of worry and fire, but seeing him eases some of the panic rolling in my stomach. If something happens, at least Dan knows who to go after.

"Show me," he says, and I turn the phone around so he can get a look at Aleric.

"Is this your boyfriend?" Aleric asks and comes down the steps.

"Yes," Dan says, and I get a little thrill. Not sure if he's saying that as a ploy to protect me or if he means it. Dan and I have been through a lot, but he vowed to give me time to figure out who I am without him before we talk about us.

"I would have thought you'd call your father."

"Oh, I'll call her dad even if she doesn't." Dan sounds cold, and it makes me shiver. Dan and that sword of his are downright lethal.

"This is Aleric Buchard."

"It's Nathaniel. I don't think anyone but my father called me Aleric."

"What do you want?" Dan goes right to the heart of the matter.

"Just to meet my sister." Nathaniel frowns, clearly not expecting so much hostility. "That's all."

Three girls pass by us, openly staring. So not the best place to do this. "Come on, let's go sit down." I walk past Nathaniel up to the porch and take a seat at the first bench.

He follows and sits beside me, close enough so Dan is able to see us both in the camera's field of vision. "I really mean no harm. My grandparents wanted me to wait until they could determine if you posed a threat to me or not."

"Me, threaten you?" I give him my best what-the-heck look. "Georgina was going to sell my soul to buy her freedom from a debt owed to a Fallen Angel incurred by *your* family, and they think *I'm* a threat?"

"What?" Nathaniel asks, the confusion

110

plain as day all over his face.

"They didn't tell you that, did they?" I let out a harsh laugh. "Go ask them about their dealings with Deleriel, especially Georgina."

"I don't really know Georgina, outside of the fact she's my mother. She showed up out of the blue at my grandparents' house while I was away at school. I only met her over the summer, and even then, I think we only talked about ten minutes during that whole time. The only thing of interest she told me was that I had a sister."

"Your family…"

"Is no worse than yours," Nathaniel finishes for me. "Both our families deal in dark magic. I was raised in both white and black magic and use both as I need them. It's who I am, and I won't apologize for it. Doesn't mean I'll ever use it against you, though."

I want to believe him, but my past has taught me not to trust easily. Family or not, he has to earn the right for me to trust him.

"Where's your sister?" Dan asks, breaking my line of thought.

"She went over to Wade's."

"Sister?" Nathaniel frowns. "I didn't know your father had another child."

"He doesn't." I tilt the phone so I can see Dan a little better. "Mary and her family took me in and gave me a home. She and I went through some stuff. You don't go through what we did without coming out the other side of it as family. She may not have my blood in her veins, but she's my sister in every other sense of the word."

"Mary." Her name rolls off his tongue in his thick Georgia accent. It's quite charming. I make a note to myself to keep Mary away from him. Not that she'd fall for his southern accent, but still. I'd rather not take that chance. I'd hate to have to hurt my own flesh and blood if he did something to her.

"So, I have two sisters now," Nathaniel muses. "More to worry about."

I frown, and he laughs.

"If she is your sister, then she's mine

too. The Buchards take care of their own."

"Are you sure that's all you want?" Dan asks, bringing our attention back to him. "Her own father contemplated sacrificing her to gain her gifts."

"But he didn't because she's his flesh and blood." Nathaniel's eyes harden. "I may not have known about my sister very long, but I was raised that family is the most precious thing in the world. We're all we have in this life, and we'd kill to protect each other. She is safe with me."

"But is she safe with your grandparents?" Dan counters, and it makes Nathaniel pause. Something shifts in his eyes.

"Would your grandparents be willing to sacrifice me for my gifts?" I pull out The Voice, the one that lets no one lie to me.

"Yes." Nathaniel slaps a hand over his mouth. "I mean…"

"Would you hurt me to take my gifts?" I push harder.

"No, you're my sister. I won't hurt

113

you."

"Even if it means you can gain the gifts of both a demon and a god?"

"What?" he whispers, his face paling.

"Would you murder me to gain those gifts?" I put all the power I can drum up in the question, forcing an answer out of him.

"No."

Dan lets out a breath, and I relax. For now, Nathaniel is convinced he won't hurt me. Down the road, that might change. Heck, it might change later today once he thinks about it, but in this moment, I can relax.

"I don't understand…" He shakes his head as if to clear it. "What did you do?"

"It's one of my gifts," I say and smile for the first time since I met him. "No one can lie to me. Not even my father."

"That's…useful." He looks dazed, and I can't blame him. Not being able to lie to someone is usually a choice, but in our line of family friends, it is useful.

"Squirt, I have to go. We're at a crime scene. If I don't get a text from you every ten minutes, I'm calling Zeke."

"I'm good, Officer Dan. Go play detective."

"Every ten minutes." He gives me that patented Officer Dan cop look I can't mimic no matter how hard I try.

"Promise."

"Love you, Squirt."

"Love you too." I disconnect the call and smile.

"Squirt?" Nathaniel asks.

"It's a nickname he gave me when I first met him two years ago." I scoot away from Nathaniel slightly, but he notices.

"I really won't hurt you."

"I know." I nod. "At least you won't right now. You may change your mind later."

Nathaniel frowns. "Why would I change my mind? You're my family."

"I just…" I stop, not sure what to tell him.

"Just what?"

"How much do you know about me?" I finally ask him.

"Only what Georgina told us. She said you were Ezekiel Crane's daughter, and she'd left both of you when you were a baby."

"That's one way of putting it." The shortest version of the truth if there ever was one.

"Why don't you tell me what she didn't?"

"I have a better idea." This is not a conversation I want to have on the front steps of my dorm where anyone can eavesdrop. "Why don't you meet me at my father's house, and we'll all sit down and talk tomorrow? I have something I have to do tonight, or I'd take you straight over there now."

"I was hoping you'd let me buy you dinner, and we could talk."

Not sure I want to go anywhere alone with him even though I know he's not lying about wanting to hurt me, but one thing I've learned is people who are supposed to love and protect me don't always do that. Hazard of growing up in the foster care system.

"I promised I'd go help with a ghost hunt."

"Ghost hunt?" He cocks his head like I do when I'm turning something over in my mind. "You inherited your father's reaping ability?"

"You know about that?"

He smiles. "Yeah, both families know all about each other. It pays to know the strengths and weaknesses of those who can hurt you."

Truer words have never been spoken.

"The Dubois and Crane families are two of the most dangerous in the supernatural world, Emma. We need to know how to defend ourselves, should one turn against the other."

"And if they do, then what?" I ask. "Would you come after me or my father?"

He purses his lips. "I won't hurt you."

"But my father? My grandparents?"

"I don't know what to say. If they came after me, I'd be forced to defend myself."

"But if your grandparents ordered you

to go after them first?"

"It's a moot point. There's been peace in our families for more than fifty years."

He skirts around the question, but really, what did I expect? It's a hard question.

"Tell me about your ghost hunt." He twists so he's facing me again. I decide to let him change the subject. He and I need to get to know one another before we start with the difficult stuff.

"It's a house that's occupied by a soul eater."

He winces. "That's rough. Those things are a beast to put down."

"You know how to put them down?" He might be of some use after all.

"Not directly, only stories I've heard." His hazel eyes twinkle at seeing my excitement.

Dang it. Here I thought we'd be able to make the house safe for the baby without all the effort of trying different things.

"And it requires the use of dark magic."

And there go the rest of my hopes. I

will not use dark magic. The demon half of me snarls at my refusal, but I won't feed the darkness that lives in me. It's too dangerous.

"We'll find another way." I sigh. I should know better than to assume anything in my life will ever be easy.

"I'm sure you will." He leans his shoulder against the bench. "I'm only here for the weekend. I have classes I need to get back to, but I wanted to meet you. I was hoping we could spend some time together, get to know each other, but I understand your hesitation. If you showed up at my dorm unannounced, I'd be wary of your intentions too."

"I'm not really good with the whole family thing," I tell him. "I'm just getting used to having one."

"What do you mean?"

"It's a long story, but I grew up in foster care. I just met the Cranes last year."

He frowns, his hazel eyes troubled. "I don't understand. Georgina said…"

"She lied." I roll my head, trying to

relieve the ache settling in my neck. My head is pounding, and I need to find some Motrin. "I've had a rough day, Nathaniel, and it's going to be an even rougher night. I need some sleep before I go back into that house. I know you're not here for long, but if I don't get some Motrin and my bed soon, I will not be responsible for what occurs. I do want to talk to you. I have since Silas told me about you, but I need a clear head to do that. Can we talk tomorrow at Zeke's? Please."

"Why don't I come with you on your ghost hunt instead?"

Uh…hard to keep him away from Mary if he goes with me, and then there's Doc. He gets hives thinking about my dad. What would he do if I showed up with a member of the second most dangerous family in the south?

"Ummm…"

"I just want a chance to get to know you, Emma. I'm pretty good with the supernatural. You never know, I might be able to help."

I shouldn't…

I know I shouldn't, but…

"Okay. Be here by six. Mary's gonna pick me and Eric up. You can hang out in the van with me. Doc wants to see what he can see on the cameras and get more information before we come up with a plan to oust the little bugger."

"Doc?"

"Dr. Lawrence Olivet."

"The Spook Doctor." Nathaniel nods. "I've heard of him."

"Everybody's heard of him." I stand and hope it's a not so subtle hint to get him moving.

"Six o'clock?" He stands and shuffles from foot to foot.

"Yup."

"Can I hug you, or is that too weird?" He's looking everywhere but at me, and it gives me a second's hesitation. Why is he so nervous? Is he planning on trying to pluck a strand of hair? Having that could give him a lot of power…

Stop it, I tell myself. *Not everyone is looking to hurt you. He came here of his own free will, against his grandparents' wishes.*

Are you sure?

I want to strangle that little voice in the back of my mind, the one left over from my foster care days that won't let me trust in people.

I choose to ignore it. I'm going to believe he came here to meet me with no intentions of hurting me. I might be wrong, but I hope not.

"Sure, you can hug me."

He finally looks at me, and I see my own uncertainty reflected in his eyes. He's just nervous because, well, we've never met, and it *is* awkward.

I'm the one who hugs him first, and he lets out a sigh when his arms go around me. It's weird, not like when I hugged Zeke for the first time. That felt easy and like I'd finally come home. This feels…not bad, but not like home either. There is a strange connection, like we recognize each other as being from the same flesh and blood, but it isn't an instant bond. Maybe it will come with time; maybe I am holding back because I don't trust him.

The truth will out itself in the end.

But for now, I'm going to attempt to get to know him and be wary at the same time. It's the best I can do.

We say our goodbyes, and I go to my room in search of Motrin and my bed.

Fire.

Flames consume every surface. It licks at the wall, pulls air from oxygen-starved lungs. The heat is intense as I try to find my way through the darkened house. I can hear the cries coming from the nursery, but the faster I try to run, the more the pain assaults me.

Looking down, I can only stare in horror as the flames crawl along my legs, latch onto my flesh, and blacken the skin until it resembles ash. My baby screams, and I ignore the pain, trying desperately to reach him before the flames can take him from me

"Wake up!"

I snap my eyes open, my fist lashing out and connecting solidly with flesh and bone.

"Oww!" Mary screeches, holding her shoulder. "What did you do that for?"

"Sorry." I sit up, rubbing my eyes, the memory of the dream already beginning to fade. "Bad dream."

"You and your need to hit people who wake you up," Mary grouches, but her tone softens. We both have nightmares that could cause anyone to strike blindly upon being abruptly wakened.

"Hey, at least I stopped sleeping with a knife under my pillow." After everything that happened, I needed to feel safe when I first came to New Orleans. Having a knife close to me so I could defend myself helped. It scared Zeke and the grandparents, but once the therapist told them I needed it, they backed off. Took me months to feel safe enough to put the thing back in the kitchen where it belonged.

"Thank God for that," Mary mutters.

Yawning, I look over at the clock. It's already after six. Great, I slept through the alarm.

"Hey, there's a guy downstairs who says he's waiting for you?" Mary rummages through her dresser drawer looking for something. "Know anything about that?"

"Dark brown hair and hazel eyes?"

Mary nods, pausing in her search to look over at me, curious.

"That would be Nathaniel."

"Who?"

"Alreric Nathaniel Buchard."

She frowns. "Why does that name sound familiar?"

"Because he's my brother."

Wait for it…

"*Your brother!*"

Clearly, I'm not the only one who had a bad reaction to my brother showing up on our doorstep. I hate to think what Zeke is going to say when I bring him by the house tomorrow.

"Yup."

"Why is he downstairs waiting for

you?" She makes a beeline for the bed and falls backward on it, staring at the ceiling and trying not to freak out. She's heard as much about the Dubois as I have.

"Because he's coming with us tonight."

She bolts upright, her big blue eyes so wide I think they might explode. "Have you lost your freaking mind?"

"Maybe." I shrug and get up to shuffle to the bathroom. I have sewer mouth, and I hate it. Fuzziness on my teeth is one of my top five most hated things.

Not deterred, Mary follows me to the bathroom. "You do realize his family is why you were in that whole mess to begin with?"

I brush my teeth before answering her. "The key words being 'his family.' He didn't know anything about that."

"How can you be sure?" Mary persists. "Even the Cranes didn't want you near him."

"Because I used my Voice on him, Mary. He can't lie when I do that."

"Unless he can." She narrows her eyes. "What if he has the same spell that lets you and Dan lie to Zeke?"

The thought has crossed my mind, but I'm choosing to believe he's not lying to me. Stupid, but it is what it is. If he's lying, I'll deal with it.

"He's only here for the weekend," I say as I go back into my room and start to rummage for clothes. I'm going for all black. It seems appropriate for hunting ghosts. Yes, I know I've seen far too much *Ghost Adventures*. Black is a staple for them.

"It doesn't matter how long he's here, Mattie!" Mary shouts, losing her patience and reverting to my old name. "He's dangerous."

"And he's still my brother." I turn to face her. "He's my family, Mary, same as you and Eric. I just want to talk to him, and I thought I could do it around the people I trust the most. Neither of you will let him hurt me."

Mary shuts up, and I use her silence to slide back into the bathroom to change clothes. Mary knows I have trust issues, so when I use the T-word, it means something.

It only takes me a minute to change and run a brush through my wild hair. Some days I hate curls, especially with the humid heat in Louisiana. It's always fuzzy and untamed. Sighing, I grab a scrunchie and rejoin Mary, who's busy texting.

"I'm ready."

She ignores me and continues to text. Must be Wade.

"I'll be outside when you're ready," I say and start toward the door. That gets her attention.

"Oh, no you don't!" She grabs the back of my long sleeve shirt and yanks me. Not hard, but with enough force to stop my forward motion. "You are not going anywhere near this guy without me or Eric."

"Then, can we go? We're already late. Doc hates to be kept waiting, even if the Scooby Gang doesn't care."

"Would you stop calling them that?"

she asks, exasperated.

I shrug. I call it like I see it.

She shakes her head and grabs her purse, pulling out the little wallet with her ID and debit card. I keep mine in my glovebox, another thing she's always pestering me about. It's not safe, what if your car gets broken into…yada, yada, yada.

We're both quiet as we go back downstairs and outside to where Nathaniel is waiting. He's leaning against the wall, watching the people who are out walking. He turns his head as soon as he hears us step out, a small smile playing on his lips.

His eyes zero in on Mary, and I can tell by the slight way they widen, he was not expecting her to be my sister. She's light to my dark, all that blonde hair and blue eyes.

"Nathaniel," I greet him, "this is Mary."

"We met earlier." He wipes his hands down the side of his pants before extending one to Mary. "Hello, Mary."

She eyeballs his hand like he's the devil instead of my brother. I nudge her, and she grudgingly shakes his hand.

"If you do one thing to hurt my sister, there will be no place on this plane or any other you can hide from me, understand?"

Mary's voice is as quiet as Zeke's when he's in threatening mode, and it causes her to sound super scary. Go, Mary. I didn't know she had that in her.

"Perfectly." Nathaniel keeps his smile in place. "I only want to get to know her. I've always wanted a brother or a sister. It's lonely being an only child."

Mary tenses, and I wonder if she used to think that before I came into her life. She'd been an only child for almost nineteen years. Her mom worked as a nurse, sometimes night shifts. How many times had she come home to an empty house or gone to bed without another soul around?

"Well, let's go. We need to pick up Eric." I nudge Mary again as she's standing there, staring. I'm not sure about her expression. It's one I've never seen before. I'll have to ask her later what is going on in that head of hers. "Are you riding with us or taking your own car?"

"I can ride with you, if you like."

Awkward car ride with my potentially murderous brother, or listening to Mary harp on and on about how this is a bad idea? Easy choice.

"Mary's riding shotgun. You can sit in the back with Eric."

Mary shoots me a scathing glare, which I ignore and head to my assigned parking spot. It's going to be a long night.

Eric is waiting outside his dorm, talking to a girl I don't know. She's pretty. Short, blonde, and overly flirty. She's leaning in just a little too far so Eric has no choice but to look down her shirt. Rolling my eyes, I honk the horn.

"Who's that?" Mary whispers.

"No clue."

Eric says something to the girl then comes over to my car, getting in the back seat. He gives Nathaniel a once-over.

"Nathaniel, this Eric."

They bump fists as guys tend to do.

"You look like Hathaway." Eric leans up and flips the radio on.

"Hathaway?" Nathaniel looks lost.

"I haven't told him everything." I turn the radio back off. My head is still killing me. Not as bad as before, but enough that the noise sets off jackhammers in my skull.

"In a nutshell, she was kidnapped, given the name Mattie Hathaway, and then ended up in foster care. Her family found her, and now she goes by Emma Crane, but I refuse to call her that. She's Mattie to me."

Nathaniel blinks. Several times. I know because I keep glancing at him in the rearview mirror.

"How long were you in foster care?" he finally asks.

"I grew up in the system. Zeke found me a little over a year ago."

Nathaniel is quiet, as are the rest of us as we drive back to the Duchaines'. I can't even guess what he's thinking.

133

Whenever anyone discovers I'm a foster kid, they get weird. I don't know why, but almost everyone does this. It's like they pity me, but at the same time, they don't want to. I was hoping to put off telling Nathaniel any of that until tomorrow at Zeke's, but thanks to Eric's big mouth, that's a bust.

All I can do now is answer any questions he has and hope he doesn't pity me or judge me.

I have a feeling our already long night just got longer.

There are two vans parked in the Duchaines' driveway when we pull up, forcing me to park on the sidewalk, something I hate to do. The small fortune Zeke dished out for this car gives me hives, and the thought of anyone scratching it—well, let's just say nuclear warfare is a mild reaction.

"The Ghost Chasers?" Nathaniel does his best to keep the laughter off his face, but he doesn't manage it. Mary shoots him another hostile look.

"What about it?" she snaps.

"Uh…" Nathaniel stares at the van, trying to find something nice to say, but there really isn't. It's a cheesy name.

"You guys are late!" Wade shouts from the front porch.

"Your sister doesn't like me very much, does she?" Nathaniel asks when Mary hurries up the steps to greet her crush.

"I think it's more she's worried about the danger you might pose to me. She's protective."

He laughs softly. "Yeah, I got that right off. Mary reminds me of a lioness."

"If you think she's a lion, you don't even want to contemplate what I'm like when it comes to protecting my family." Eric's quiet words startle us both. I didn't realize he was right behind us.

"I'm not here to hurt her, I swear." Nathaniel turns to face him, his expression earnest.

"That's what a lot of people who ended up hurting her said. I won't ever let that happen again. I'll kill you first, and her father will make sure it's never tied back to me. Are we clear?"

Eric's deadly threat is even scarier than

Mary's. He means it. I see it in his eyes. He would kill to protect me the same as my father would. It's probably why Zeke likes Eric so much. He sees how much Eric loves me and the lengths he would go to in order to keep me safe. I should be shocked and appalled, but I'm not. It gives me a sense of peace knowing how much I mean to him.

"Crystal," Nathaniel says, his voice neutral.

"Now that all the threats are out of the way, let's go see about getting this thing out of the house for this family." I start walking, cutting off any further conversation.

Doc is standing in the living room, directing traffic. There are all kinds of equipment covering nearly every surface. Cameras and microphones are going up, as well as equipment I can't even name.

"Doc?"

He turns and gives me a tired smile. "I didn't know if you were coming. You're late."

"Sorry about that. I slept through my

alarm. Nasty headache."

And just like that, he goes into concerned parent mode. He knows all about the seizures that almost killed me during the Deleriel adventure.

"How bad is the pain? Where is it? Should we get you to the ER?"

"Why would you need to go to the ER for a headache?" Nathaniel comes to stand next to me, curious but concerned.

"It's a long story and one we don't have time for. I'm fine, Doc. Just a regular headache. Nothing to worry about."

Doc doesn't look like he believes me, but he lets it drop. "Who is this young man?"

"This is my friend, Nathaniel. He knows quite a bit about the supernatural, and I thought he might be able to help." Doc knows about the Dubois family and what they're capable of. No need to spring on him who Nathaniel actually is unless it's necessary.

"You're interested in the supernatural?" Doc quirks a brow at my brother, waiting for his response.

"You don't grow up in Savannah without learning all about the ghosts that roam the area. It's one of the most haunted cities in the States."

"Yes, it is." Doc nods approvingly. "I've studied quite a few hauntings there."

"What's all this?" I sweep my arm to encompass everything going on.

"Seth and I got here early and managed to get our cameras up in the best positions, and now I'm making sure they don't get taken down or swapped while these boys put up theirs."

Sneaky, but I expect nothing less of Doc.

"What about the rest of this stuff?"

"Various things. Some are mine, some are the boys'. We need to study the environment, so we are monitoring heat signatures, cold spots, trying to get all the scientific evidence we can to back up what we already know is here."

"The boys being the Scooby Gang?" Nathaniel deadpans, and I check to make sure Mary didn't overhear before letting out a small laugh.

Even Doc chuckles. "I'm not sure they actually know what they're doing, but they have invested in some nice cameras."

"Rich kids with too much time on their hands," I mutter. Eric hears me and nods. We both know what it's like to be poor as paupers.

"Aren't you a rich kid too?" Nathaniel asks.

"Technically, but I don't act or think like one. My dad gave me a credit card, and I get hives when I think about it. I'm content without a lot of money."

"Okay, everyone, I think we're live!" Wade calls, and I turn to see a bank of computer monitors showing every room in the house except for bathrooms. One screen shows heat signatures, each room represented on the squares of the screen. It looks professional, and I grudgingly admit I might have to give some props to the Scooby Gang.

"Uh, what now?" Eric leans over my

shoulder to stare at the screens. "We just sit around and wait for something to happen?"

"Pretty much." Ethan sets down a bag of cameras as he comes into the room. "A lot of this is watching and waiting."

Eric's entire body freezes up. I can feel it because he's pressed against me trying to get a better look at the computer screens. He really likes this guy, even if he doesn't want to admit it. I'm not going to push him on it the way Mary does. I understand what it's like to wake up with strange and unsettling new feelings coursing through you, feelings you didn't ask for or want. I'm not going to make him any more uncomfortable than he already is.

"Why don't we gather in the dining room and go over our information?" Doc suggests and ushers us toward the side entrance off the kitchen. The archway flows into a very large dining room with a table that could easily seat fifteen or twenty. It's made from old mahogany, something I only know because of Zeke.

He was gushing over his office desk he found at an auction. The desk and the table look to be made of the same type of wood.

Once we're all seated, Doc lets Wade do his thing first.

Wade stands and clears his throat, moving to the head of the table. He looks at us, trying to build atmosphere, I'm guessing. It only makes him look awkward.

Once Ethan hits record on his camcorder, Wade begins. "After speaking with the Duchaines at some length, we have determined they do indeed have a haunting. They are experiencing classic signs of hauntings such as lights flickering, cold spots, the water faucets in the house turning on by themselves. They've also heard things like footsteps on the stairs at night. Our job tonight is to capture physical evidence of the haunting and potentially identify the ghost who is still hanging around. Sometimes, if you can confront them with their identity, you can get them to move on. We've set up gear throughout the house that will help us get what we need and what may deliver this family from the horror they are suffering."

It takes everything I have not to say something snarky. This guy actually has followers on YouTube who listen to this? No personality at all.

Doc takes Wade's place next, and I sit back. At least we might hear a good intro for the Scooby Gang's video on this haunting. Doc has the kind of voice that draws you in and keeps you hanging on his every word. He's a born storyteller.

"Thank you, Wade," Doc nods and shuffles through the papers he's holding. "My assistant Seth did most of the work here by going to the library and digging through a lot of old records."

The guy, who's three chairs down and across from me, tips his head in Doc's direction. He looks to be about Nathaniel's age, but he's got sandy-blond hair and green eyes. A strong jaw and very elegant nose complete his face. He's cute.

"This house was built in 1956, along with every other house on the street. Before that, the land belonged to one Christopher Harcourt. His family ran into some financial trouble and had to sell off everything they owned. It was not something the family wanted to do, but it was a choice between eating or living on the streets."

He clears his throat and looks around the room, his gaze resting on each of us in turn, and we all lean forward, his voice pulling us in as he weaves his tale.

"There have been three suspicious deaths on this property. One was Amelia Harcourt, the wife of Anderson Harcourt, who bought the land back in 1843. The death certificate ruled her death accidental, but it's hard to accidentally break your neck in your own living room."

Last night's dream comes back to me, and I wonder if any of the suspicious deaths were caused by fire.

"We fast-forward thirty years to the death of Graham Harcourt, the youngest of son of Anderson. He drowned in the lake that is attached to the property. Accidental again. There were no clear details on the drowning, so we don't know exactly the method of drowning."

I am so done with water deaths. I still can't take a bath because of the ghost who tried to drown me in the tub.

"And our last death occurred in 1972, when the father of the last owner of this house died. Henry Duchaine passed peacefully in his sleep. As you can see, there are no flashing neon signs screaming at us as to why this house is haunted. Those deaths were abrupt, yes, but not violent."

Drowning was a violent death. Not being able to breathe? Yup, it'll scar a person for life. I know it for a fact.

"Was there ever a fire on the property?" I ask, trying to get my mind off the memory of drowning.

"Yes," Seth says. "In 1922, the original estate caught fire, but it was during the summer, and the entire family was away."

"Was there anyone else in the house, though?"

Seth cocks his head and stares at me, his eyes unreadable. "I don't know."

"We might want to check that. Fire is as violent a death as you can get. It might have been the hired help who died here."

"So noted." Seth scribbles something down in his notebook.

"Now we travel in time to our clients, who inherited the house," Doc continues, bringing our full attention back to him. "The new owners put everything they had into updating the home and fixing the problems that arose. I'm thinking all the renovations disturbed our sleeping ghost, which seems to have targeted their little girl. Our goal here is to study, yes, but also to remove the ghost from this home so there is no more danger to the child or her parents."

See? Basically the same thing Wade said, but delivered with much more *umph*. Wade has a lot to learn before he can be anywhere near Doc's league.

"So, what's the plan?" Eric leans

146

forward, his elbows propped on the table.

"Ethan and I will walk through the house, trying to get the ghost to talk to us, while Jordan monitors everything from our hub of operations." Wade stands, nodding to Ethan and Jordan. "Dr. Olivet, would you care to join us?"

"Thank you, Wade, but I have my own process." Doc smiles indulgently. I notice he doesn't invite the Scooby Gang to join *him*.

"Mary, why don't you and Eric help Jordan out?" Doc suggests, and I'm grateful. I don't want my sister or Eric wandering around in this place after what happened earlier. At least here they might see what's coming for them on the heat signature monitor.

"Sure thing, Doc." Mary plops down next to Jordan and gives him a bright smile, which causes a permanent blush on the poor kid's face.

"And, Emma, you and Nathaniel can monitor everything from outside. That way if anything goes wrong, we have someone who can call for help."

Mary and Eric frown, neither of them wanting me to be alone with Nathaniel. I'm not sure I want to be alone with him either, but there's not a lot to do about that unless we want to 'fess up to Doc and the Scooby Gang.

"Come on." I head back toward the front door before anyone can try to find reasons to keep me inside. I really don't want to be in here. That soul sucking ghost took a lot out of me, and I'm not looking forward to facing her again.

It's quiet as I exit into the early evening heat, something I'm entirely grateful for. Because of all the ghosts, I'm eternally cold. New Orleans helps dissipate some of the cold so I'm not freezing all the time.

I make a beeline for Doc's van and open the back doors to see a technological mess. I have no idea what half this stuff is, but it's lit up like Christmas. Monitors line one entire wall, and a pull-down bed is clipped to the other. Equipment is all over the floor.

"Wow. He means business, doesn't

he?" Nathaniel lets out a whistle when he gets a good look at the inside of the van.

"I guess so." Looking around, I spot two headsets and plug them both into the spot marked as audio output. Doc explained all this to me before we left, thankfully. I hand one of them to Nathaniel. "We're supposed to keep an ear out for anything unusual, or if they scream for help."

He takes the headset but doesn't put it on. "Have you ever done this before?"

"What?"

"This." He waves his hand around the van. "Go out hunting ghosts."

"God, no." I have enough trouble with ghosts coming to me without seeking them out. Although if I see a ghost like the kid on the roof, I try to help them. It keeps the reaper in me from going stir crazy.

"Then how did you get roped into it?" He quirks a brow the same way I do when I'm curious. It's disturbing.

"My sister likes Wade, who's in charge of the Ghost Chasers." I can't keep the snicker out of my voice. "She didn't want to come alone when she met the rest of his crew for the first time. Bunch of strange guys…well, let's just say we're both smarter than that. We grabbed Eric and met the guys here, only to discover the family had called in Doc too."

"You know him well?" Nathaniel puts the headset on but leaves his left ear bare so he can listen to the house and talk to me at the same time.

"Yeah. I met him back when I was still in foster care. He helped me understand what being a living reaper actually meant."

"But you don't trust him."

That gets my attention, and I look over at him. He's watching me, his hazel eyes intense. "Why would you say that?"

"Body language. It's something my grandparents had me studying for as long as I can remember. Yours says you don't trust him, at least not completely."

Huh. I'll have to ask Zeke about that and learning how to control my reactions. I don't like anyone being able to read me.

It's safer that way. The less people know, the less they can hurt you.

"Doc and I have had our problems, but we're working it out."

"You said earlier you grew up in foster care? How did that happen?"

I let out a long sigh. I should have guessed he wouldn't wait until tomorrow.

"I was kidnapped by my nanny when I was about two. She died when I was five, and I went into foster care until Zeke found me when I turned seventeen." That was the long and short of it, minus the major details.

"I'm surprised she was able to hide from your father for that long. He has ways of finding what he wants."

"And my mom had ways of countering them." I let a small smile slip out. I used to hate Claire, but then I realized everything she did was to protect me. She loved me in ways no one else ever could.

"So, you still think of her as your mother?" Nathaniel sat on the van floor, and I followed suit.

"Yeah, she's the only mother I've ever

known, and she loved me."

"I don't think Georgina would be what you'd call mother material." Nathaniel shifted, trying to get comfortable.

"That's an understatement."

Before he can ask anything else, we hear Wade begin his spiel by asking if there's anyone there.

Nathaniel and I both roll our eyes, but we do shut up and listen. We are supposed to be monitoring everything, after all.

But we both know it's going to be a long night.

As I suspected, it *was* a long night. My watch laughs at me when I see it's after four in the morning. Nathaniel dozed off, and I let him sleep. It kept me from having to answer more questions. At least he'd stopped asking such personal ones when he saw I wasn't going to give him more than the most basic of answers. I don't trust him. I want to, but my instincts have never been wrong, no matter how much I would like to believe otherwise.

The screens have the boys still wandering around, trying to get the ghost to talk to them, while Doc and Seth have set up shop in the baby's room. That is a smarter move, even though the ghost hasn't shown up yet.

Which is strange. One would think she'd surface for air and pitch a fit because her food supply is gone. Or maybe she's waiting us out, knowing the family will come home eventually. I don't know if this is the first time she's struck or not, since Doc's assistant didn't have a lot of time to really dig into the history of the place. Maybe I'll go look at the library tomorrow too.

I laugh at myself. Me, actually thinking about going into the library to dig through old records. Don't get me wrong; I like to read. It's a new habit I picked up, but I read on my Kindle, and I get to stay out of libraries. Not my favorite place to go. I've run into a few nasty ghosts in libraries before.

Maybe I can sweet-talk Mary into doing it. She likes libraries. Something about the smell of old books. My nose wrinkles at the thought. I do not like the musty smell that permeates the air in libraries.

The ache in my back is getting worse. It comes from having my butt plastered on the floor all night. Glancing at Nathaniel to make sure he's not awake, I take off the headset and silently let myself out of the van so I can stretch.

It's quiet. All the houses on the street are dark, a few with porch lights burning against the silky strands of the night. An owl hoots in the distance, breaking through the silence that crowds the street.

Now that I think about it, I don't hear anything on this particular street. No cats or dogs, no scurrying of little creatures, no crickets. There's not a sound to be heard except for my breathing. It shouldn't be this quiet out here.

My gaze sweeps the street, taking in both sides, looking for any signs of life, but there are none. It has to be the ghost, or what used to be a ghost. I'm honestly not sure what it is now, except an entity full of rage and bent on revenge.

She must be around here, or the animals wouldn't be hiding, but she's not showing herself to anyone in the house. Something that angry, it makes no sense it would hide from free food. The people in that house are inviting her in, trying to get her to come forward. So, why is she staying hidden?

I glance back inside the van, and Nathaniel's head is down, his chin tucked into his chest. How he can sleep right now, I have no idea. I've never been able to pass out like the dead through anything. He must get that from his dad.

Shooting a quick text to Doc, I start for the back of the house. I want to look around since the ghost has decided to crawl into her tomb and stay there. If she's not out, she's not a danger to me.

I might be curious, but I'm not stupid, which is why I texted Doc to come out back. This chickie takes no chances. When you learn the hard way, it sticks with you.

Those boys can go around holding up their static boxes that are supposed to capture voices and their EMF detectors all day. It won't do them a darn bit of good. If I'm right, we'll not get anything from her tonight.

The back yard is as neat as the front. Several small flowerbeds are sewn around the deck and two big willow trees that give the back yard ample shade. A swing set and one of those wooden playhouses sit under one of them. An overturned tricycle sits in the yard alongside a kiddy pool.

If not for the silence, it would be an average, ordinary backyard.

The back door squeaks open, and Doc slides out, looking behind him before closing the door. The Scooby Boys have been trying to insinuate themselves into his investigation, but he's proven adept at keeping them at arm's length. Points to Doc for that feat. Those guys are persistent, if nothing else.

"What's up, Mattie?"

Doc also refuses to call me Emma when no one else is around. Not that I blame him. He's known me as Mattie since I was at least two. I still haven't gotten around to discussing that picture I found of me and my mom, Claire Hathaway, in his briefcase. Maybe one day I'll give him the opportunity to tell me about it, but that's a long way down the road.

"What's wrong?" His brown eyes are wide and watchful.

"You tell me." See if the Spook Doctor hears what I do.

A big nothing.

He cocks his head, trying to figure out what I know that he doesn't.

It's very telling to watch him work through the problem. He studies everything with a sharp eye I'd attribute to being a trained police officer, but Doc is an investigator. I can see him run through the gambit of possibilities then discard each one until he lands on the truth.

"It's silent as a tomb out here."

I nod. "Yup. I thought it was a little odd. I mean, there's noises, but nothing on this street. I think our ghost has either scared them all off or eaten those brave enough to take a stand."

"It's not the wild west, Mattie." A rueful smile catches at Doc's lips.

"Well, it kinda is, though," I argue. "The supernatural is a realm not many believe in, let alone try to fight. Those of us who do are the lawmen."

"Let me guess, you plan on opening your own Pinkerton Detective Agency for the supernatural?" He says it jestingly, but it sparks an idea. An idea I would have run away from two years ago, but not now.

Dan always tells me I'll make an excellent cop. As if I would ever join the police force. Cops and I don't get along. Never have, never will.

But a private investigator?

Now, that's something to think about. If I can connect with all the hunters out there fighting on their own, we might be able to pool resources and actually do something and back each other up. It could save lives.

Too many die from trying to fight alone. Even when we're not alone, sometimes we still die. Eli is a case in point. He was on my side. He died to protect me. I still wonder if there was something I could have done, should have done.

Nope, not going there right now. Focus on the case at hand.

"The ghost is hiding." Best to steer him back to the case too. If he gets any ideas I'm thinking of opening my own agency when I graduate, I can hear the lectures now. As excited as Doc is about my abilities, he's very much against anything that puts me in real danger.

"I don't believe we'll be getting anything tonight." Doc rolls his head to relieve some of the stress. "Seth has been taking recordings all night in the nursery, but even the temperature is normal."

"Has anyone gone down in the…"

That's when we hear the screaming.

The basement.

Doc and I burst through the back door right off the kitchen. The basement door is tightly closed.

Mary comes rushing into the kitchen, her face white as a ghost.

"What's wrong?" I grip her hands in mine, trying to calm her down.

"S…Sethhh," she whispers.

"Seth?" Doc's face pales. "What's wrong with Seth?"

Mary shakes her head and bursts into tears. Doc doesn't waste another second. He takes off running and nearly knocks Eric over in the process.

"You should go help Doc," Eric says

and takes Mary from me, wrapping her in his arms. "The guys are with him, but…"

I don't waste another minute and take off running right behind Doc. The house, which had felt empty earlier, is pulsing with energy. The ghost is awake.

Seth is sprawled on the nursery floor, his face a chalky white. He's unconscious, and his breathing is shallow. Not only that, but the ghost is attached to him. I don't think anyone else can see her, but I can.

I jam my hand into my pocket and pull out the small pocketknife I carry, the blade made completely of iron. Dan had it made for me. It's small enough to carry with me, but not big enough that anyone would consider it a threat.

But this ghost is going to.

I push Ethan of out my way and stab the thing right in the neck. When it doesn't move, I do it again. This time, she hisses and turns to look at me.

Uh-oh.

Maybe I shouldn't have poked a violent, soul sucking ghost with the equivalent of a stickpin.

She grins, recognizing me. I bet I taste way yummier than Seth. I'm full of ghost energy, the next purest thing to an infant soul.

The boys are all looking at me like I'm crazy, but Doc's gaze is sharper. "It's her?"

"Yeah, and she's pissed." I take three steps backward, and the ghost follows me, mimicking my every movement.

An idea takes hold, and I take several more steps, drawing her as far away from the others as I can before I open my own nuclear weapon.

Without even thinking about it, I open a circle to The Between around her, effectively trapping her. She snarls at me, and it's my turn to grin.

Gotcha, Ghostie.

"What the…?" Wade whispers. "The EMF is spiking off the charts."

"Did you…?" Doc cocks his head while trying to rouse Seth.

"I did. It's the only thing I could think of to trap her, or did you want me to let her go back to snacking on Seth?"

"Of course not, but you can't leave that open indefinitely."

"Sure, I can. I used to sleep with it open around my bed."

Doc stares at me incredulously. "Did your teacher never explain why that's not a good idea?"

"Uh, no?" I don't recall ever telling Kane I did that, but now is not the time to play confession with Doc. He'll only yell at me.

Doc shakes his head. "Boys, go call an ambulance."

When Wade looks ready to argue, Doc gives them a stare that is worthy of my old social worker, Nancy Moriarity. I miss her.

"Fine, but I have questions that will be answered." Wade stares pointedly at me.

"I'm sure you do, but right now we need to get medical attention for Seth. He's not waking up, and that is concerning."

Frowning, I leave the murderous ghost in her trap and go over to kneel beside

Doc's assistant. He's not waking up. In fact, he's as eerily silent as the street. Sure, he'd moaned when the ghost let him go, but he'd fallen so still and quiet. Just like the street.

"This is my fault."

"No, it's not." Doc runs a hand over his eyes. "He knew the risks…"

"She was hiding when everyone was paired up, but I called you outside, leaving Seth alone. It's what she was waiting for."

Doc's mouth falls open in a silent O. He hadn't thought of that yet.

"Daniel is right. You're going to make an excellent police officer," he finally says. "You're always thinking three steps ahead."

"Never happen, Doc."

"We'll see." He turns his attention back to Seth. "His pulse is weak."

"Remember Jonah?"

"How could I not? That was a very eventful adventure."

Eventful adventure…try psychotic nightmare that still haunts me. "When he was draining me, I felt tired, and all I wanted to do was sleep. To just give in and go to sleep. What if that's what she does? Makes them sleep until she's drained her victims?"

"Then why isn't the baby…? Because she wants to savor Hailey. Her energy is the purest thing in this world. Of course, she'd want to feed on her for as long as possible."

I need help. "Kane!"

It only takes a few seconds for him to appear. He looks tired when he pops in beside me. Can reapers get tired?

"You rang?"

"Now is not the time for sarcasm," I say and gesture to Seth and then to my trapped ghost. "We need some help."

"What did you do?" His eyes are wide and fearful. "Mattie, you put a soul eater where she has unfettered access to souls?"

"What are you talking about?"

He grabs my head and turns me to face the ghost. "Look, Mattie, really look."

When I look, I understand why she

didn't pitch a fit at being trapped. I locked her in a prison where she could eat unfettered. She's pulling energy directly out of The Between, and I can see the souls inside her, both those of the lost and the wraiths, giving her more and more power. She's bloated with it.

"No," I whisper, horrified. "I didn't know…I swear I didn't know."

"Get everyone out." Kane stands. "We have to cut off her food supply, and no one living can be in this house when that happens."

Realizing Doc can't see Kane, I repeat his instruction. "Take Seth and get Mary and Eric out. I have to stay and fix this."

"Mattie, you just said that no one living can be here."

"I'm not really human, though, am I, Doc?" I give him a rueful smile. "My soul is made up of more ghost energy than anything else. Besides, I made this mess, and I have to fix it."

"I don't know about this…"

"Go on, Doc. The ambulance should be here soon, and I don't want anyone coming in while we defuse the bomb."

And that's exactly what she is right now. She's full of energy and more powerful than any ghost I've come up against. She could do some serious damage.

"Okay, but promise me you won't do anything stupid."

I smile and give him a mock salute. Not promising that, because I probably will do something stupid.

Once he's gone, I turn back to Kane, who's eyeballing the soul eater with trepidation.

"How do I fix this?"

"I don't know."

Well, that's not good.

"If I tear down the circle, she gets out, and I'm betting she'll wreak havoc."

"She may have enough energy to break her ties to this house." Kane walks the circle, studying her much the same way Doc studied the back yard earlier. "If she gets into the outside world, unfettered, there's no telling what damage she'll cause."

"Or who'll she'll hurt." I finish the thought for him. "We can't let that happen."

"Well, duh." He gives me a look that says the same.

Sometimes I wonder exactly how old Kane is. There are times he speaks like a teenager, and times he speaks like he's as old as my grandfather.

"Have you ever reaped a soul eater?"

"God, no." A full body shudder wracks him. "Reapers stay as far from these things as we can get."

"Why?"

"Because while your soul may be made up of mostly ghost energy, ours is nothing but ghost energy. That thing would devour me the minute I touched it."

Not good, not at all.

"So, how the heck are we gonna defuse her?"

"No clue." Kane shrugs and stands there, staring.

Out of desperation, I call someone I haven't spoken to since I left Charlotte.

"Mattie?" Caleb Malone picks up right when I think it's going to go to voice mail.

"Hey, Caleb." The words come out low and strangled. He sounds a lot like Eli on the phone.

"Is everything okay?"

"Uh, no. It's not."

"Tell me."

Just like that, the awkwardness goes away. Caleb never blamed me for Eli's death. None of his family did. Eli was my Guardian Angel, and as such, if dying was his only way to protect me, then they understood.

I explain everything I know and what I did, and how it backfired on me.

Caleb lets out a low whistle. "You done gone and got yourself into a pickle, didn't you?"

"Yeah, but I don't know how to fix it."

"And you said your reaper friend can't just absorb the soul?"

"Even if she wasn't all hopped up on wraith juice, he still couldn't. She'll latch on before he even has a chance to run. He has no protection against…" Holy crap!

"Mattie?" Caleb prompts when I fall silent.

"Uh, Caleb, I might be able to defuse her, but I can't force her to cross over. It has to be her choice, and I'm betting she's not gonna want to do that."

"How can you defuse her if a full-fledged reaper can't?"

"Silas sort of gave me a new tattoo that stops her from snacking on me. I forgot until just now because of everything going on here at the house, Mary starting to date, Nathaniel showing up…"

"Wait, Mary's starting to date?" Caleb's voice gets a little high. I close my eyes and bow my head. I shouldn't have said that. Caleb has a thing for my sister, but he chose to stay in Charlotte and follow in the family business instead of what he really wanted to do. Mary let him go, but I'm not sure Caleb ever let her go.

"Now is not the time, Caleb." I clear my throat. "Is there a way to kill it outside of a blessed blade?"

"No." His voice gets very quiet. "You can't just kill a ghost with any old thing. It would be easier if you could."

"Can we trap her somehow that doesn't involve The Between?"

"That's the question hunters have been asking for centuries, and we still don't have an answer." He lets out a long sigh. "Maybe I should come down there with my sword?"

"No." Mary would have a conniption fit. "I don't think that's a good idea, and I need to learn to handle these things myself. I just wanted some advice."

"I wasn't very helpful."

"You were, actually. You made me remember my new ink."

"You're going to need to text me the design so I can incorporate it into our library."

I'd do that. If I can help save even one life, I will.

"Do you know any hunters in New Orleans you trust, Caleb? In case we need backup?"

"I thought you said…"

"Caleb."

"Fine, I know a couple, but if Dr. Olivet is there, I'm sure he knows more hunters than I do…"

"I don't trust him, Caleb, but I do you."

Caleb was quiet for a heartbeat. "Okay, Mattie. I'll have them call you at this number, yeah?"

"Thanks, Caleb."

"You're very welcome, and don't wait to call until you're in trouble. You're family, and I miss you."

"I miss you too. Do me a favor?"

"Yeah?"

"Call Officer Dan and tell him not to freak out, that I'm just going to exercise my reaping abilities, and I'll call him later tonight, okay?"

"You want me to lie to my brother?" He might sound all surly, but I can detect the hint of laughter in his voice.

"I'm not lying. I'm going to go in and reap all the souls she ate. I've done it once before."

"And it almost killed you."

"But it didn't."

"Just be careful, okay?"

"I will. Talk to you later." Hanging up before he can say anything, I push the phone back into my pocket.

"What tattoo are you talking about?" Kane stalks over and demands to see.

I lift up my pants leg and show him the still covered tattoo. "Silas did it earlier when Miss Piggy over there decided I was lunch. He says he can't have me dying after all the work he did to save me."

"Let me see it."

"Nope. Silas said to leave it covered until at least tomorrow. I'm not going to ruin the design because you want to see it."

"What's the plan, then?"

"I'm going in there with her and pulling the souls out of her."

His face goes ashen. "You really are insane."

"She can't feed on me like she can you. We can't release her until she's powered down. You have a better idea?"

174

"No, but that doesn't mean I like this one."

"No one said you had to like it."

He shoots me a glare but stops arguing. He knows I'm right.

I look at Miss Piggy, as I've named her, and she stares at me, daring me to come to her.

This is going to hurt.

Here goes nothing.

13

"There's something you should know before you get in there." Kane's words sound ominous, but I try to not let it bother me as we make sure the cameras in the room are off. I do not want this showing up on YouTube. I've already texted Eric to cut the audio feed, which I'm sure is going to make Wade furious, but I refuse to be the next YouTube spectacle.

"The souls that thing is syphoning from The Between are wraiths."

"Yeah, I know that."

"No, you don't understand. Wraiths have turned ugly and twisted, their souls black. They're evil. If you reap them, all that darkness gets reaped into your soul as well."

"And?" I wish he'd get to the point instead of dancing around what he's trying to say. I'm already nervous enough.

"And given your demonic heritage, I'm worried."

There's no denying the fear radiating off Kane. Nothing ever fazes Kane. He's a rock in a sea of sharks. But I can hear it in his voice. He's afraid.

"So, what you're saying is if I reap all those wraiths, I'll turn evil or something?" I have to force the words out. Maybe I should tell him my demonic side woke up this morning.

"It's possible."

Fudgepops.

"But if we don't do it, this ghost is going to get out, and that'll cause a whole mess of other problems. I won't put anyone else's blood on my hands, Kane. I have enough of that already."

"There's more." Kane's words are so

low I almost miss them.

"More?"

He nods and shuffles closer so his mouth is pressed right against my ear and begins to whisper. "My bosses are still watching you. They already know your demonic side woke up. If this causes all your abilities to reawaken, there's a good chance they'll do what they were going to do last time."

My eyes widen. Kane's bosses were going to allow me to use all my gifts from both my demonic grandfather and my metaphysical mother, who just happened to be a goddess, to defeat Deleriel. Then they planned on taking me out. I'm not supposed to exist in this world, anyway, and neither is Dan. We're unnatural, and they're afraid of what I can do if I learn to harness all my gifts.

I swallow thickly. Suddenly, my mouth feels full of sawdust. There are very few things that scare me anymore, Silas being one of them, and Kane's bosses being the other. I'd never see it coming. They could just pass judgement, and it would be over before I could blink.

I've survived too much to die now.

Especially at the hands of some bureaucratic supernatural government.

"What's going on in here?"

Both Kane and I whip our heads around at the sound of Nathaniel's voice. How did he get in here? I told Doc to keep everyone out.

He's drawn right to where my ghost is trapped.

"What did you do, Emma?" His eyes are wide, but there's no fear there. He looks more impressed than horrified.

"I trapped a soul eater."

"With a circle of The Between. Gutsy." He walks around the circle. "But how are you planning on getting her out now that she's pigged out on wraiths?"

It shouldn't surprise me he knows all about The Between, but it does. I guess I figured the only people who know about it are living reapers like me, and there aren't many of us out there.

He gives me a sheepish smile. "It pays to know everything about the supernatural when you run in our circles."

I guess that is true enough, but I don't trust his words. As much as I want to, I just don't. I hope he proves me wrong.

"You should probably go back outside with the others. When she gets out of the circle, she's going to try to find someone to munch on to regain some of her strength."

"I'm protected. She won't be munching on me."

"Protected?"

He nods. "My grandparents warded me against everything they could think of. There's not a lot that can get past my defenses."

Good to know, in case I have to be one of the things that gets past his defenses.

"But what about you? Are you protected?"

"Yes," I say and look back to the ghost, putting my worries about Nathaniel away for the minute. I need to get this done before the ambulance gets here. "Can you stand out of the way, please? Protected or not, I don't want to have to worry about you and me both."

My eyes flicker to Kane, and he nods. He's ready if I need help, even if that might get him killed. It's good to have friends who have your back, no matter what.

"Is there anything I can do to help?" Nathaniel asks, his eyes glued to the ghost.

"Just stay out of my way."

Taking a deep breath, I force my legs to move and walk over until my toes touch the edge of the circle.

Cold.

The Between is the coldest place I've ever visited. There's no heat at all. It's a desolate place of unforgiving nothingness.

That's what seeps up out of the circle and wraps around me. At first, I fight it because it reminds me of being trapped, unable to move, but then I remember Kane's lessons.

The Between is made up of everything I am. It's cold and stark, like death. I am death. All reapers, living or not, bring death to souls. We convince them to move on, instead of clinging to the last trappings of their lives. Death isn't unkind or cruel. It's simply the natural succession of life. Souls are meant to move on from this life to the next.

Once I remind myself I am the cold, it stops scaring the bejesus out of me. I embrace it and step over the circle and into the ring with Miss Piggy the soul eater.

She snarls and reaches for me, and I don't flinch. Her hands wrap around my upper arms, and she tries to latch onto my soul. I can feel her rooting around, trying to catch the broken, shattered strands of my soul.

But she can't.

When she realizes she can't, I finally smile. The one I reserve for people who piss me off, the one full of teeth and the promise of pain.

She tries to flee, but there is nowhere to go. She's trapped. I can feel the hatred oozing out of her, but I pay it no mind.

Instead, I open up that part of myself that is a reaper. It only takes a moment to find it.

Without warning, the ghost shrieks and flies at me, knocking me backward and out of the circle. I land with an audible thump.

That stung.

"Your eyes…" Nathaniel whispers, his voice a little awed.

"Never seen a living reaper before?" Kane asks and startles Nathaniel so badly he stumbles backward.

"Who are you, and where did you come from?" My brother looks a little pale. I'm guessing people don't get the jump on him easily.

"I'm Kane."

"A little help here?"

Kane leans down and helps me to my feet. "You okay, kid?"

"Yeah. My hip took the brunt of it. I'll be fine."

"Back to my question. Have you ever met a living reaper before?" Kane turns his attention back to my brother.

"No." Nathaniel looks from me to Kane. "Do their eyes always glow like that?"

"Only the most powerful ones. Your sister is the strongest I've ever met. Most stubborn too."

"Hey!" I am not that bad.

Kane gives me a cheeky grin in reply.

"Let's focus on the ghost and not on my stubborn streak." I glance back at the ghost, irritated. She'd gotten the jump on me, and I don't like it. Not one little bit.

"Can you collect them from this side of the circle?" Nathaniel keeps his eyes on Kane, still not sure who he is and why he's here.

"If that was the case, I'd already have done that," Kane tells him sarcastically.

"Nathaniel, Kane's a full-fledged reaper."

Something slithers behind his eyes. If I hadn't been staring straight at him, I'd have missed it. It's something dark, and it sets off internal alarm bells.

"Hey, Kane. Can you come over here and stand next to me in case I need help?" I motion to the opposite side of the circle, the side farthest from Nathaniel.

Nathaniel's face is deceptively blank, but I think he knows I saw something I didn't like. Just one more reason to be cautious.

Kane frowns but does as I ask. Once he's safely away from Nathaniel, I take another deep breath and step back into the ring. Round one went to Miss Piggy, but I'm going for the knockout round.

She's on the offensive the second I'm in the circle, but this time I'm ready for her. I push my reaping powers out, imagining long ropes reaching and binding her. Wispy white cords form and latch onto the ghost, holding her.

The minute she realizes she's bound, she starts to fight me, twisting and turning, doing everything she can to escape.

I turn inward, closing my eyes and tasting the air around me. The scent of death is everywhere. She's so old and angry, she stinks of rot and decay. Rage has eaten her alive. There's nothing left of the woman she was.

At least, not that I can find. To help her, I need something that belonged to her or something that would be familiar, anything to reawaken even a whisper of a memory of who she was.

That's something to worry about tomorrow. First things first. I need to defuse the nuclear weapon about to explode. I raise one hand, palm outward. I can feel the trapped souls inside her. They're scared and angry, but they're also evil. Hungry. Starving, really.

Wraiths are scavengers in The Between, all of them fighting over the random lost soul that accidentally finds its way into The Between without a guide. And I do mean rare. Only a reaper can open a doorway to that plane. Sometimes souls get scared, break away from their guides, and get eaten before the reaper can do anything.

So, the wraiths starve for who knows how many months or years at a time. It's the hunger I'm feeling in the pit of my stomach. Gnawing pain that demands to be fed.

"Don't get lost in the emotions." Kane's voice breaks through the fog starting to cloud my mind, and I shake my head. These things are dangerous, even housed within Miss Piggy.

Time to get this done. I plunge my metaphysical hand inside the ghost and feel for the souls. They flock to my light like bees to honey. As I consume them, my skin begins to crawl and itch. It feels like some icky, dark substance is inching its way up my arm. Heavy, dark molasses, the kind my grandmother uses to make her gingerbread cookies. I remember turning the bottle up and watching it ooze out into the bowl. That is exactly what this feeling reminds me of.

Without warning, hundreds of images assault me. I can see how each soul I consume died. Some were ordinary deaths, but most were horrific ones. These souls did awful things in life and ran from death, only to end up as a hollow shell. If they weren't such evil creatures, I'd feel bad for them.

With each soul lost, my ghost loses more and more of her mojo, and her struggles are getting fainter and fainter, until there's only her left. I've got her in my hands, holding her broken soul, one as broken as mine.

There is no fear. Only hate. She wants nothing more than to destroy everything she touches. I could take her soul apart, shred it into nothingness. The ability lives within me, but then I remember Kane's warning. His bosses are just waiting to use the smackdown on me. I'm not going out like that.

Instead of ending her, I drop the circle of The Between and let her go. She flees instantly, heading straight for Nathaniel, but like me, she bounces off him. He *is* protected.

"Your eyes…" Nathaniel takes a step away from me.

"I was afraid of this." Kane slides to the right, trying to put himself between me and my brother.

"Her eyes are black."

"That's because I'm part demon, same as you." Really, the pot shouldn't call the kettle black.

"You know about that?"

"Didn't you just tell me we should know the people who have the ability to destroy us?"

"Yeah." He tries to smile, but it falls flat. "My eyes have never done that, though. No one in my family has demonic eyes."

"I'm special that way." I turn to Kane. "How do I get these things out of me? I'm having some strange and disturbing thoughts."

"Like what?"

"Like how I have this gnawing hunger to consume you, Kane."

My hands shake with the effort not to grab him. It wasn't so bad a minute ago, but the longer these things are inside of me, the need gets stronger and stronger. The ick has slithered up my arms, around my shoulders, seeking an entrance. I need these things gone, like, yesterday.

"Give them to me." Kane holds out his hand.

"Won't these things do the same to you?"

"No, they won't. I don't have a human body anymore. I can house them and return them to The Between. Give them to me."

That's all I need to hear. Taking his hand, I open myself up and let him leech the little suckers out of me, but when he does, all my energy goes too, and before long, another darkness overwhelms me, and I sink into the oblivion of unconsciousness.

The first thing I hear when I finally wake up is arguing. My headache is gone, at least, but I feel like I've been on a three-week bender. My whole body hurts, and I'm sick to my stomach. No headache is a major plus, though.

"How do we know he didn't do something to her?" Mary tries to whisper but fails miserably.

"Kane said he didn't," Eric says, sounding more agitated than I've heard him in a while. "He said she'll wake up when her body's ready to, and not until."

"I'm right here, you know." I can hear the exasperation in Nathaniel's voice.

"I know," Mary retorts. "I'm just not talking to you until I hear from my sister that you didn't do something to her."

"She's my sister too," Nathaniel rebukes. "I wouldn't hurt her."

"That has yet to be proven," Mary tells him. Boy, does she sound pissed.

"He didn't do anything." I force my eyes open and find myself staring up at the ceiling in Doc's van.

"Oh, thank God," Mary breathes and is beside me in seconds. "I got so scared when you wouldn't wake up. Don't keep doing that to me, Mattie."

"Mattie?"

I turn my head to see Nathaniel frowning. Of course, he has no idea or he's a very good liar, but it takes one to know one, doesn't it?

I am an exceptional liar, and I think my brother and I share that.

"My name was Mattie Hathaway when I was in foster care," I explain and sit up. "Remind me never to take in that many souls again. It hurts like nobody's business."

"What happened?" Mary asks, fussing like a mother hen.

"Didn't Nathaniel tell you?"

"Well, yes, but I want to hear it from you."

I smile ruefully. Leave it to Mary to go into overprotective mode. She has good reason, though. I've almost died more times than I can count.

"I trapped Miss Piggy in a circle of The Between, not realizing she'd gorge on the wraiths. She was a ticking bomb, and we had to defuse her. Kane couldn't because she'd suck him dry, so it was up to me. I took in all the souls she ate before letting her go. Only that many souls is not so good for me. I guess it knocked me out after Kane took them all from me."

"See?" Nathaniel raises a brow in an I-told-you-so manner.

Mary shoots him a disdainful glare in return.

"Miss Piggy?" Eric cracks a smile, but it does little to hide the worry on his face. I scared him. I think this is the first time he's seen me pass out from a ghost experience. Well, aside from when he was a ghost and accidentally almost killed me.

"She was sucking up wraiths like a pig. What else should I have called her?" I try to smile, but even my face hurts. "How's Seth?"

"Dr. Olivet rode with him to the hospital," Mary says, finally calming down. "We told him we'd text him as soon as you woke up."

"Already done." Eric holds up his phone.

"What time is it?" I ask, rolling my shoulders to try to get some of the stiffness out of them. Not sure if it came from my ghost adventure or the hard bed I'm sitting on.

"It's a little after five in the morning." Mary yawns. "I'm beat."

"Let's go to Zeke's and crash. Mrs. Jones should have breakfast ready soon." My dad's cook and housekeeper is the best. I adore her chocolate chip pancakes.

"Can you drop me at my hotel first?"

Nathaniel asks. "I'm pretty beat too."

"You can crash at Zeke's too." Might as well rip that Band-Aid off sooner rather than later.

"I can't, Emma." Nathaniel frowns. "How will he react if I show up unannounced?"

"He'll deal. Now, let's get out of this cramped van and go partake of some chocolate chip pancakes."

"I love those." Nathaniel's eyes light up. Well, he has good taste in breakfast, at least.

"Me too." I give him a slight smile, and we all pile out of Doc's van, Eric making sure to lock it up tight before pocketing the keys, and then climb into my car.

The ride to Zeke's is quiet. We're all exhausted, and I know Nathaniel and I are both preparing for my father's reaction to him. Let's just hope Zeke doesn't try to kill him on sight.

My father lives outside of the city in a sprawling plantation home. It's a functioning plantation too. Zeke grows crops like a regular farmer. I think it's cotton, but I've never really bothered to find out. Farming holds zero interest for me.

The house, on the other hand...that, I adore. I love historic buildings. It's the artist in me. I've got sketch pads full of drawings of the house and the outbuildings. The architecture is divine with its sweeping columns and wide steps. The three-story structure is white with red shutters and a red door. It's been very well taken care of. Zeke said he bought it about ten years ago and restored it to its full glory. He's a bit of a home improvement buff. He did a lot of the restoration work himself.

We turn into the long driveway lined with weeping willow trees right up to the beginning of the gardens. From there it's clear of trees all the way to the front door. Mary and I tend to park right in front of the steps, and someone always moves the car later.

My father's butler, Jamison, greets us as we come in. He doesn't even look surprised to see us. Nothing ruffles him.

"Good morning, Miss Emma." His smile could defrost the frozen tundra. "I hope everything is okay?"

I yawn around my answer. "Fine. Just got done with a ghost hunt."

He raises his eyebrows but doesn't comment. "I assume you're all starving?"

"Yes." Eric shuts the door behind him. "We are starved. I hope Mrs. Jones doesn't mind us tagging along."

"Of course not," Jamison replies. "She loves a full house." His eyes stray to Nathaniel.

"Jamison, this is Nathaniel." I don't add his last name for fear he'll rush upstairs and wake Zeke.

"Good to meet you." Jamison smiles and continues toward the kitchen. "Come along, and I'll let Mrs. Jones know you're all about to die of starvation."

My stomach lets out a loud grumble of agreement, which prompts a lot of laughter. It's not like I can control the bottomless pit.

Nathaniel sticks close to me, making

me think he's nervous about being in the same house with Ezekiel Crane. Given what he's told me about our families, he's probably wondering what Zeke is gonna say when he finds out who Nathaniel really is. I'm hoping things won't go sideways, but with my luck, they probably will.

Mrs. Jones is humming when we get into the kitchen. She looks like she's barely awake, but she's as chipper as if she's been up for hours. If I didn't adore her, I'd have to hate her on principle. Morning people need to be drawn and quartered.

"Good morning, children." She gives us her best smile, ignoring our grimaces at the word *children*. "I was told you're starving. How does hash browns, pancakes, and eggs sound?"

"Chocolate chip?" I ask, taking a seat at the breakfast table.

"Of course." Her crooked smile is on full display. "Regular for Eric, and blueberry for Mary, and..." Her voice trails off when Nathaniel sits beside me.

"This is Nathaniel. He'll have chocolate chip too."

Mrs. Jones is a lot shrewder than Jamison. Her eyes settle on my brother, and he shifts uncomfortably under her scrutiny. Her gaze bounces between us, and I see a flare of recognition before it clears. She knows exactly who this is.

"Of course. I just need to go do something, and I'll be right back. Emma, why don't you grab some drinks for your guests."

"Two guesses where she's going." Eric slouches in his chair, yawning.

"I only need one." I get up and head to the fridge. "I hope you're ready to meet Zeke, Nathaniel."

"I'm really not." There is a bit of panic in his voice. "I'd rather he get used to the idea before he meets me."

"Mrs. J is on her way up to wake him." Eric takes the pitcher of OJ I give him and sets it down. "She pegged you the second she laid eyes on you."

Zeke comes rushing into the kitchen a few minutes later. His gaze lands on me, checking to make sure I'm okay, and then settles on Nathaniel.

"Hey, Papa." I stand and go to hug him. "We decided to come crash here after our ghost hunt."

"You mean after you passed out cold," Eric reminds me, and I groan. Did he have to lead with that?

"What happened?" Zeke asks, brushing his longish brown hair out of his face. He always reminds me of the actor who plays Ichabod Crane on Fox's *Sleepy Hollow*. It's not any one thing; he just looks like him. I swear they could pass for twins.

"A soul eater is terrorizing a family. We were trying to figure out a way to get it out of the house when I trapped it in a circle of The Between. Long story short, I had to fix the problem I made. Drained me a little, but I'm perfectly fine. Just starved and bone tired."

"Emma Rose, you are not well enough yet to be taking on soul eaters." If it isn't for how worried I know he is, I'd say something snarky right about now. He loves me, so he gets a pass on trying to tell me what to do. I'll do what I want anyway, but he doesn't have to know that.

"It all turned out okay." I shrug and go sit back down. "Papa, this is Aleric Nathaniel Buchard, my brother."

"Yes, I do know who he is, *ma petite*, I just don't know why he's here." Zeke takes the last seat at the table beside Mary.

"I came to meet my sister." Nathaniel doesn't show a bit of the nervousness he had a few minutes ago. Brownie points to him for that. My dad can be intimidating.

"Out of the blue, though?" Zeke's stare could freeze an Eskimo. "Why now?"

"Because I only found out about her two weeks ago." Nathaniel clears his throat and sips at his orange juice. "Georgina told us about her right before she left. My grandparents wanted me to wait until they had time to scope out the situation, but I wanted to meet her, so I booked a flight and did just that."

"So you say." Mary's glaring at

201

Nathaniel like he's the devil.

"You don't believe him?" Zeke turns his head in her direction.

"I don't know, but I do know what you told us about his family, and I'm not going to let him hurt Em."

"Neither am I," Zeke assures her.

"I'm not here to hurt her." For the first time all night, some of his frustration starts to shine through. "I just want to get to know my sister. That's all."

"Are you sure that's all you want?" Zeke dials up his Voice, the one that can get the truth out of almost anyone. "You're not planning to kill her and take her gifts, are you?"

"No, sir. I just want a chance to be her brother. She's my family as much as she is yours. I want the same opportunity you have."

Zeke's nostrils flare. Nathaniel passed the test, but that means bupkis. There is a way to get around it. I never told Zeke that, though, and I'm not about to tell him now. I love my dad, but a part of me, the part that lived in foster care for so long, still needs a way to protect myself. Even from the one person who loves me more than anyone in the world.

"Zeke, if he wanted to hurt me, he could have done it earlier tonight. I was alone with him and Kane in the house. Nathaniel carried me out of the house when I passed out. He didn't try anything shady."

Still not sure if I believe him, but I want Zeke to stop throwing daggers at him.

"I don't want you alone with him, Emma Rose." He takes the morning paper Jamison hands him. "Not until I'm reassured he means you no harm. If the two of you want to get to know each other, then do it here where I can watch him."

"I have a plane to catch in the morning, but I thought maybe we could have dinner?" Nathaniel gives me a slight smile, knowing Zeke may not trust him, but he didn't forbid me from talking to him. Not that it would matter if he did, but still. It's nice to be able to make the old man feel good.

"I wanted to talk to Papa about trapping Miss Piggy anyway, so maybe between the three of us, we can come up with something. Dinner would be good."

"Miss Piggy?" Zeke frowns. "Isn't that a Muppet?"

Eric snickers, and even Mary has to turn away to keep from laughing at his confusion. I spend the rest of the morning telling him all about the soul eater, what happened to Seth, and the nuclear reactor she became.

At least one good thing came out of the day.

Zeke didn't murder Nathaniel on sight.

Tomorrow, though? Could be a different story altogether. I'll just have to wait and see.

My eyes blink open, and I shake my head. Sitting up, I throw the covers back and slip off the bed, my bare feet coming into contact with the cold wooden floor beneath me, making me shiver.

An uneasiness creeps over me, and I frown, looking around my small bedroom. Something isn't right. I can feel it in my bones.

There doesn't sound like anything's amiss, but something disturbed my sleep. I check the baby's crib, but he's sleeping soundly.

We're alone tonight, the other servants having been given the week off. Mr.

Lewis, the butler, said he'd be back before dawn to help with the household chores. He knows taking care of the baby and the house wears me out.

I pull my robe on and open the bedroom door, listening. It's as silent as a tomb. Glancing back at the baby to make sure he's still sleeping, I make my way out into the hallway and down the stairs. I'm sure I locked up, but it's never a bad idea to double check the locks. It wouldn't do to have someone break in and steal the family I work for blind, especially on my watch.

Mrs. Harcourt already hates me. My son is her husband's illegitimate child. He refused to let me move out. He wants his child raised in his father's family home. Who am I to argue? My son will have an education and maybe marry into a better status than the one he was born into. I can keep my lover's wife away from my boy while suffering the brunt of her wrath myself if it means a better life for him.

Downstairs is as quiet as above. I blew

the gas lamps out before retiring for the night, so instead of bothering to light them again, I use one of the candles on the hallway table. It'll be more than enough light to see by since the moon is out and there are lots of windows in the manor.

Perhaps I was disturbed by something in a dream. Everything looks in order down here. The house is still locked up tight. Maybe some warm milk will help to settle my nerves enough to go back to sleep.

The kitchen is dark, but the glow from the fire slumbering in the cookstove along with the candle is enough to allow me to make my way to the icebox and retrieve the glass bottle of milk. I find the teapot and add the milk to it before setting it on the stovetop. It's still warm enough to heat the liquid without having to stoke the fire.

Yawning, I start to turn around when a noise catches my attention. I stay still, listening for it. It sounded like footsteps, but that can't be right. I'm alone in the house.

Or maybe Mr. Lewis came back early?

"Mr. Lewis?" I call softly, almost afraid to raise my voice. What if it's not him? The doors and windows are still locked. I checked. No one could get in without a key. It has to be Mr. Lewis if someone is in the house.

The footsteps come into the kitchen, and my hands start to shake. There is someone in the house. Turn around, *I order my stubborn feet, but they won't move. Fear has frozen them in place.*

"Hello, Matilde."

He knows my name! Who is this?

"Did you really think she'd allow him to keep his bastard child in this home with her?"

Oh, God. This is Mrs. Harcourt's doing. She hates my son because she's been unable to give her husband a child. She's sent someone here to kill my baby, to kill us. I won't let anyone harm my son.

My feet unfreeze, and I take off running, my only intention to get to my baby. Cruel fingers twine in my hair and pull me backward against a wide chest.

"Oh, no, you don't." His breath stinks of liquor and rot. "You're not getting out of here alive, little one."

A sharp, stabbing pain assaults my middle, and I look down to see him pulling a knife out of my stomach. He plunges it in again and again before letting me fall. The pain is debilitating, and I can't move. All I can do is watch as he walks out of the kitchen and listen as he goes upstairs.

To where my baby is sleeping.

***

Unknown number.

It's called my phone three times in ten minutes. I typically don't answer calls from people I don't know, but this incessant ringing is getting on my last nerve.

"What?" I finally snarl into the phone. I'd been napping, something I really need to do if I'm going to go back in the ghost's den. I'm still so tired I can barely hold my head up.

"Well, hello to you too, *cher*."

"Who is this, and why are you calling my phone?" I grouch around a yawn. Really, did he need to ring the house down at the godawful hour of noon?

"My name is Cass Willow. Caleb Malone asked me to call you. Said you might have a ghost problem?"

Crap on toast. I completely forgot about that.

"Sorry. You woke me up. I don't function well without sleep."

"No worries, *ma cher*." He has this silky-smooth voice only a life-long resident of New Orleans possesses. His French accent rolls off his tongue. "I've been known to murder for less."

"I do have a ghost problem, but it's a little more serious than your run-of-the-mill ghost who's gone dark."

"Do tell."

"It's a soul eater."

His gasp is evidence he knows what I'm talking about. "I'd say you have more than a problem."

I snort. That's putting it mildly.

"She's so full of hate, there's no way I'm going to be able to convince her to move on, so we might need some help to force her."

"We don't have a blessed blade. My cousin Jimmy is up north with our only one, dealing with a rather nasty ghost victimizing children in an elementary school. Not sure when he'll be back. Let us do some research, and we'll meet up tonight at the site of the haunting. That sound good to you, *cher*?"

Well, dang it. I need a blessed blade. Not sure how else to deal with Miss Piggy otherwise, but I hope this guy can help. "Yeah, that'd be great. I'm all out of ideas."

"Text me the address, and I'll see you around nine tonight."

"Sure," I say around another yawn. "And thanks for helping on short notice."

"It's all good. It's what we're here for."

I thank him one more time and hang up

211

the phone. The bedside clock mocks me. Barely three hours of sleep. I'm not going to be able to get back to sleep, though. Once I'm up, I'm up. Bad habit I picked up when I was ten. Never did break myself of it.

Mary's passed out next to me, having slept like the dead through all my grouchiness. Eric's sprawled at the bottom of the bed. That boy could sleep through an earthquake.

They both refused separate rooms when we decided to try to sleep. They said someone needed to watch me because of what happened earlier, and Zeke agreed. Though, to be fair, neither of them will wake up unless I scream the house down. They are out.

Slipping out of the bed, I stumble as the dream I'd been having flashes in front of my eyes. I know exactly what it is. It's Miss Piggy and what happened to her. I had been inside her pulling souls left and right. That isn't done without seeing into her head a little.

What happened to her and her baby

was horrible. I'm guessing the man set the house on fire to cover up the crime. I understand why she's so angry and how that anger turned to rage, but it doesn't give her the right to torment innocent little babies because hers died.

I'm quiet as I do my business in the bathroom then sneak out of the room, leaving Mary and Eric still sleeping. The first person I go looking for is my dad. He's easy to find. The only place he ever really goes is his office.

He's arguing with someone on the phone when I knock. He waves me in, and I flop down on his very cushy couch facing the windows with a view of the gardens. I love the gardens here. They're overflowing with every flower imaginable and have been the inspiration for more than a few of my drawings.

"I don't want any more excuses. Just get it done." Zeke slams the phone down, and I glance at him askance. That didn't sound good.

"Everything okay?"

"No. One of our food shipments to

213

Africa disappeared. There were also vaccines in that shipment the children in that village needed. My people are telling me they can't do anything, and I told them to get it done. I want that plane found."

My dad does a lot of charity work no one really knows about. He supplies food and medicine to villages in countries that have nothing. I found out about it when he gave me an overview of what the Crane Corporation does on a global scale. I'm not the least bit interested in taking over the business, but Zeke insists I know the basics.

"That sucks."

"Indeed." He shoots another glare at the phone before turning his attention to me. "How are you, *ma petite*? Eric told me you were out for quite a while, and you had a headache."

The very idea of a headache terrifies my dad. I'd almost died from brain seizures caused by my full-on reaping abilities combined with the demonic side of my heritage.

"It's gone now. I think it was a stress headache, no big deal. Normal people do get headaches, Papa."

"But you're not normal, Emma Rose."

Now, ain't that the truth? I'd tried for so long to be normal and failed, just being me is a relief.

"I promise if I get a hint of those headaches again, I won't put it off. I'll go straight to the hospital. Cool?"

"Cool," he said drolly. "Now, what are we going to do about your brother?"

"I don't know." I pull my feet up under me and settle back against the cushions. "What do you think?"

"He's lying."

"I know."

"Then why is he here?" Zeke's blue eyes zero in on me.

"One thing I learned growing up in the system is you always keep a close eye on those you're the most suspicious of. Until I know exactly what he's hiding from me, I want to watch him."

"And here I thought you'd gone soft." The smile on my papa's face is enough to make me laugh out loud. He and I share a lot of the same ideals. We've both had runs-ins with the police, and we always come out the other side smelling like roses.

"Never happen." I clear my throat. "I hope he's not here to try to hurt me. Mary and Eric are my family, my sister and my brother, but…"

"But it would be nice to have a blood relative who loves you as much as they do?" Zeke finishes for me.

"Yeah." I feel bad thinking it because they *are* my family, and I wouldn't trade one of them for a hundred Nathaniels, but at the same time, I want a sibling who shares a part of me.

"Don't torment yourself over that, *ma petite*." Zeke gets up and comes to sit beside me. "There's nothing wrong with wanting a familial tie to someone. Mary and Eric are your family just as much as your grandparents or I. They always will be. Doesn't change the fact you want to get to know your flesh and blood. It's only human."

And there's the crux of it. I'm not sure how human I am anymore. Maybe that's why I'm clinging so hard to a relationship with Nathaniel. A relationship with my own flesh and blood reminds me I still have a part of me that's human, a part that isn't evil or a freak.

"What do you know about soul eaters?" I ask, changing the subject.

"Not a lot. I've never come up against one."

"I have." Just the memory of Jonas is enough to have me wrapping my arms around my knees. He almost killed me. If it hadn't been for Silas helping me, I would never have done it. Though I might not have defeated him. I'd put him in The Between. Granted, he'd been weak, and maybe the wraiths had gotten him before he managed to feed.

"Tell me." Zeke wraps an arm around my shoulders and pulls me close.

This is the feeling I was missing when I hugged Nathaniel, this sense of home and completeness. I can feel how much my father loves me. Zeke, like Dan, makes me feel safe. Nathaniel makes me uneasy.

I spend the next twenty minutes telling Zeke about Jonas and how it was the first time I met the Malones. It makes me miss Eli, and a heaviness settles in my heart. I loved him. Not as much as I do Dan, but I did love him. If not for Dan, I would have given Eli my heart. I used to wonder what might have happened if Eli hadn't died. I came to the realization if that had happened, the three of us—me, Dan, and Eli—would have gone through a lot of pain, and I still would have chosen Dan in the end.

"You miss him."

My father's words startle me out of my thoughts. I don't have to ask who he's talking about. "Yeah, I do."

Neither of us says anything for a few minutes. There isn't anything to say.

"Dr. Olivet called while you were asleep." Zeke uncurls himself from around me and goes to the door to call for Jamison. I hear him mutter something about orange juice, my favorite drink in the entire world. Dan always tells me I smell like the stuff since I drink so much of it.

"Did he say anything about Seth?"

"He hasn't woken up yet. He asked if you would meet him at the library to keep digging for information that might help."

Zeke laughs at the face I make. He knows how much I like libraries.

"He told you what happened to Seth?" I perk up when Jamison strolls in with a tall glass of OJ.

"Yes. He even asked me if I might have some advice on how to deal with your soul eater."

"But you didn't." I take the juice and thank Jamison before gulping down half the glass in one go.

"No, unfortunately not. I did, however, put out a few feelers."

"Caleb Malone put me in contact with some local hunters. They'll be at the house tonight for added backup."

"I am not sure I'm comfortable with you hunting, *ma petite*."

"I'm not hunting."

"Are you trying to rid a house of ghost?"

"Well, yeah…"

"Then you're hunting."

Good point.

"Well, yeah, when you put it like that, I am, but I'm only helping out on this one case."

Zeke's smile is almost indulgent. "*Ma petite*, you're meant to help people. I realized it when you took your own soul apart to save your sister. It's who you are, and despite how I feel about it, I think hunting is going to be a part of that."

"You're wrong. I came here not only to get to know my family, but to get away from who I was. I don't want to be a freak anymore, Papa."

"You are not a freak, Emma Rose Crane. Don't you ever let me hear you say that."

His outrage is palpable. Of course, he doesn't think I'm a freak. He's my father. Who happens to have the same freakish gift I do.

"You're special. The things you can do

are amazing. Why would you want to hide that away when you can use it to help so many people? To help those who can't help themselves against forces they aren't equipped to handle?"

Geez. He does have the guilt thing down. I think Mrs. Cross gave him pointers.

"I thought you wanted me to take over the family business."

"I know how much it bores you, *ma petite*. I wouldn't do that to you."

It's true. I'm an artist. Board meetings and hostile takeovers are so not me.

"You need to get married and have a son who can follow in your footsteps."

He blinks at me like I've sprouted horns. "I'm perfectly happy as a bachelor."

"Then adopt, but you need someone who loves the corporate world as much as you do."

And it would give me a brother I could trust.

"Did you hit your head when you passed out?"

221

"No, but I'm serious. You need to start dating."

And then my father blushes.

Hard.

"Wait…are you dating?"

"I wouldn't call it dating, exactly," he hedges.

"Uh-uh. 'Fess up. Who are you dating? Do I know her?"

"Well, yes."

"Who?"

"Nancy."

Nancy…my eyes widen, and my mouth drops open. "Nancy, as in my Nancy? How are you dating? She lives in North Carolina!"

"She did, but she moved here a month ago. She's now working with our child welfare department."

"And no one told me?" I shout. I can't help it. Nancy is the closest thing I have to a mother. She fought for me in the foster care system, made me realize I was worth something, and worked to make sure I was taken care of. She was what kept me alive during those first few years in Charlotte. I miss her.

"It's my fault. Nancy wanted to tell you, but I didn't know how you'd react."

"Are you kidding me? I love Nancy. Of course, I'd want to know she was here."

He winces. "I mean about us dating."

Nancy Moriarity is the one woman aside from my grandmother who keeps Zeke on his toes. She doesn't put up with his nonsense and gives better than she gets. I think the two of them hooking up is an epic idea.

"Papa, Nancy is why I'm standing here right now. If it wasn't for her not giving up on me, I don't know where I might have ended up. She's important to me. I'm not blind either. I saw what was going on between you two in Charlotte."

Again, that blush flirts with his cheeks. It's cute.

"I have no problem with you and Nancy dating. I think it's the best idea I've heard all year." Another thought occurs that dampens some of my excitement. "If you get serious, though, how do you think she's going to react to me? To us? To this whole paranormal world she doesn't realize she lives in? It might be too much for her."

Zeke's troubled expression has to mirror the one I'm wearing. "I don't know, *ma petite*. I think it's something we're going to have to play by ear."

"I guess."

"You know no matter what happens, I love you, *oui*?"

"*Oui, Papá. Je t'aime aussi.*"

"Your French is getting better."

"I have an excellent teacher." I get up and give him a hug. "I better get to the library before Doc gets lost in the stacks."

"I'll have someone drive you."

"No, my car's here. Just make sure everybody gets home, and please be nice to Nathaniel when he wakes up."

"That boy…"

"I know, but be nice anyway."

"Fine, but only for you."

Leaning up on my tiptoes, I kiss his cheek and head out. Best not to keep Doc waiting. We don't have a lot of time before nightfall, and I want to tell him everything I've learned.

I'd rather be in Antarctica wearing nothing but a bikini than walking into the public library. I can feel the cold all around me the second I step through the doors. The AC is on full blast, but this cold goes deeper. It seeps into the bones and makes your teeth ache. The place is as haunted as a battlefield.

After Katrina hit, the library suffered an extreme loss of their books, and donations from all over the country poured in, along with the ghosts attached to those items. They're not all Casper the Friendly Ghost either. Some of the ghosts that reside here now are quite angry, not only at dying, but at being displaced from their homes.

I'd be pissed too.

Keeping my head down so as not to make eye contact with any of the spirits swirling around, I make my way to the front desk and ask for Doc. The librarian, a woman in her early forties, directs me to the historical records room. Of course, it's in the basement. You'd think they'd learn not to put such sensitive information where a hurricane bent on mass destruction can get to it.

I bypass the elevator and head for the stairs instead. I've had one too many bad experiences in elevators. The morgue adventure being one of them. If I can take stairs, I do. It's easier.

Usually, anyway.

As soon as the door closes behind me, I think I maybe should have taken the elevator. The air here is dank and moldy, the dim lighting worthless. My phone's flashlight app is a lifesaver. At least now I can see as I make my way down the narrow stone steps.

A relieved sigh escapes as soon as my feet hit the floor. I was half afraid something would push me down the stairs. I keep getting a bad vibe, like something down here is very angry. I dig into my pocket and pull out my iron pocketknife. I'm glad Dan and Zeke both insisted I carry it at all times. Iron hurts a ghost and makes them vamoose long enough for me to get to safety.

The anger vibrating in the very air closes in around me as I walk deeper into the dark corridor. It's so heavy I can taste it. This thing is beyond pissed off. Three more steps, and it begins to feel like I'm trudging through quicksand. It's all in my psyche. I know this, but it doesn't do anything to help me shake it off. Ghosts are vile little creatures when they're trying to hurt you.

Fingers skim up my bare arm, and I jerk away. My sink burns where he touched it.

"You don't want to mess with me," I warn, trying to sound as mean as I can and failing. If I can hear the tremble in my voice, so can the ghost.

A hollow laugh fills the corridor.

Fudgepops.

I take off running, telling myself I'm not mired down in quicksand, but all the while feeling his heavy, rotten breath along my neck.

"Doc!" I shout and hope he can hear me. He tends to get so focused on what he's doing, he zones out, oblivious to everything else. "Doc!"

Fingers curl in my hair, pulling until I wince. It takes a strong ghost to be able to physically manipulate something on this plane. This ghost has enough anger to move a train if he wants to.

Down the hall, a door opens, spilling light out into the darkened hallway. Doc is standing there, looking alarmed. As soon as I crash into the light, the sense of dread goes away, and the ghost stops. He won't follow me into the light.

"What's wrong?" Doc looks behind me, but he can't see anything. I didn't see the ghost, but feeling him was more than enough for me to know I don't want to ever see him again.

"Ghost in the basement trying to scare me."

"Looked like it worked." Doc stands back so I can enter the room. The big wooden table across from the door is filled with books, some open, some discarded on the floor. This must be where Doc is working. There are several notepads and a voice recorder on the table too.

"A little." I rub my hands up and down my arms. It's freaking cold down here.

"Have a seat, Mattie. I have something I want to give you."

He looks so nervous it makes me curious. I take a seat in the chair in front of all the notepads. Doc's usually never nervous, and that makes me forget all about the ghost in the hallway.

Doc opens his briefcase and takes out a small square package. His fingers slide over it reverently. "I thought this belonged to you more than it did me."

I take the package and rip off the paper. Inside the white box is a framed picture of my mother, Claire Hathaway, AKA Amanda Sterling, holding me and smiling for the camera. I was a little over two in this picture. I know it. It's the same one I found in Doc's briefcase the night my best friend Megan died.

"I know you weren't ready to talk about that photo before, but I'm hoping you'll hear me out now. Even if you don't, you should have something of your mother. She loved you."

"I know she did," I whisper and trace her face with my fingertip. I remember when she came to save me last year, to help put my soul back together so I wouldn't die. Seeing her hurt so much because of how much I missed her, but I'd suffer all that pain just to spend one more minute with my mama.

"I wasn't sure how you'd react to knowing she kidnapped you, but you deserved to know how much she loved you."

"Thank you for this." I finally look up at him, and the uncertainty in his eyes is telling. He's not sure how I'm going to react. Not that I blame him. I reacted badly the first time I saw this photo, and I still haven't completely forgiven him for lying to me for months. I might not ever, but I'm trying.

"You're very welcome."

"Sit." I gesture to the seat beside me. "I'm listening."

"I met your mother in Philadelphia. She'd just moved there, and when she saw my name listed on a flyer for my first lecture, she thought it was my brother. He had a bad habit of telling people he was me."

"She knew your brother?"

He nods and takes a seat. "She'd gotten to know him while she was employed by the Cranes. He told her his name was Lawrence Olivet."

That makes no sense. "But…"

"Just let me get through this, okay?"

My mouth snaps shut. I'm confused, but maybe if I hold the questions, he can clear all that up.

"When she came to see me after the lecture, she confessed she'd met a man who claimed to be me and looked a lot like me. My brother and I are very similar, but different enough not to be confused as twins. We got to talking, and I got the whole story out of her."

He fiddles with his notepad, falling silent. Whatever is eating at him is causing him to sweat. I can see it trickling down his face.

"I have a confession to make, one I'm afraid will push you farther away from me, but I swear to you, Mattie, all I want is for you to be safe and happy."

That doesn't bode well. "Spit it out, Doc. Prolonging the torture doesn't help either of us."

"My mother met a man when she was seventeen. He put her up in a nice house, and she became his mistress. She bore him two sons and a daughter. It was years later when she ended the affair, deciding she had more self-worth than settling for being a mistress to a married man. She later married Harold Olivet, who adopted all three of us."

He clears his throat and takes a sip of

his bottled water. I'm beginning to put this together, but part of me refuses to believe it.

"I never wanted anything to do with our father. Neither did my sister, but Luke was a different story. He was fascinated by the supernatural, same as I was, but he took it farther. He started practicing the black arts and tried to get in touch with our father, who rebuffed him. He wanted nothing to do with any of us, but that didn't deter Luke. He was determined and went looking for our half-sister, Georgina, who was more than happy to entertain him. She loved to disrespect her parents. She blamed them for the mess she was in with a demon."

"Deleriel." Even saying his name makes me shake. I may have won that fight, but at a great personal cost.

"Yes. You know that story, though. Georgina never let Luke come around when your father was home, but Ezekiel traveled frequently for work. Luke had unfettered access to your nanny. He introduced himself to both Georgina and

Claire as Lawrence or Larry, as our sister called him."

"And Mom just told you all this? Told you she kidnapped me?"

"No, not at first. It took several months for her to trust me enough to confess everything that happened. She explained to me how Georgina was afraid for you, how she feared Zeke was going to hurt you and begged her to take you away. Knowing what I already did about the Cranes, I believed her."

"Only it wasn't Georgina who did that. It was my real mother who possessed her." The anger was starting to burn in the pit of my stomach. Doc had lied, but he'd kept the biggest lie to himself. For two years.

"I'm aware of that now," Doc said, his voice soft. He knew I was mad, but what did he expect? "You're upset, and you have every right to be."

"I'm beyond upset, Doc. You're telling me you're my uncle, and you thought it was okay to keep that from me?"

He lets out a heavy sigh. "I was going

to tell you, but then everything snowballed out of control. You saw the photo, then had to deal with your friend's death, and you almost lost Dan. There was so much going on. You weren't in any condition to hear the truth after you almost died defeating Deleriel. There was never a good time, Mattie. I didn't withhold the information from you deliberately or for any ulterior motive. You needed time to heal, and I was afraid dealing with this information would cause a setback. From the moment I held you in my arms when you were just a little girl, I knew my only goal in this life was to protect you. That's what I was doing this last year, protecting you as best I knew how."

The anger burns hot. I'm guessing I inherited it from both my parents. I knew if I said something right now, I'd lash out, and it would hurt him. Part of me knew he spoke the truth. Telling me before now would have caused a setback. I couldn't have dealt while trying to stitch my soul back together enough for

Dan to go home to Charlotte. I would have come apart at the seams, and I might not have ever gotten any better.

In those first few weeks after I killed Deleriel, I was so fragile I didn't even recognize myself. Every minute of every day, I felt raw, like I'd been put through a meat grinder and then dragged for miles behind a car on hot asphalt.

Doc's right. I couldn't have handled the truth then.

But I'm not sure I can handle it right now either.

"I'm sorry I hurt you, Mattie, but that was never my intention. I only wanted you safe."

"I am safe."

"Your father…"

"Loves me and would kill anyone who tried to hurt me."

Doc flinches, and I don't feel bad about it. By trying to protect me, he hurt me, even if he didn't mean to. Everyone's always hurting me that way, everyone but Mary, Eric, and Zeke. I guess I should include my grandparents in that, but I need to get to know them a little more. I run when they're around. It freaks me out having so many people care about me.

"I need time to think, Doc. I need to process…"

"Of course," he quickly agrees. "I understand that, and I can work with it."

"Tell me what you found out about the case." I sweep my hand over the open books. I can't talk about him being my uncle. Not right now. Better to focus on Miss Piggy than let my anger burn out of control. I learned to hit first and ask questions later in foster care, but over the last two years, I've slowly learned to temper my first instincts and my anger.

I need to talk to Dan about this. He— *no*. I came to New Orleans to learn to depend on myself. Running to Dan every time something comes up defeats the whole purpose. I will deal with this on my own and then tell him.

"I went to the Historical Society first." Doc shuffles through his papers until he produces a notepad. "Ah, here we are."

His voice is rough with emotion, but

he's doing better at bottling it up than I am. Brownie points to Doc for that.

"It appears the fire had two casualties, one of the household maids and her infant son. These records were not here at the library when Seth completed his search. They may have been destroyed in the hurricane. The Historical Society moved all the valuable information out of the city three days before the flooding began."

"Her name is Matilde."

"How do you know that?" He peers at me from behind his glasses. When did he start wearing glasses?

I tell him about my dream last night and everything I thought I'd learned from it.

"That certainly explains her anger, but not how to stop her." Doc runs a hand through his hair, which has more white strands than I remember. Now that I'm looking, he appears older than when I first met him by, like, a good ten years.

My grandmother once told me Zeke caused her to age quite a bit faster because of all the worry he caused her. Granted, my Gram doesn't look a day over forty, but I've seen pictures of her when she was younger. She was and still is a looker.

Doc is always telling me how much he worries about me. Maybe I'm the cause of his rapid aging.

"I called Caleb Malone earlier. He put me in touch with some local hunters who are coming to help tonight."

Doc frowns. "I could have done that. I know several."

"Caleb's a hunter, Doc. I wanted someone he would trust to watch his back. He knows more about hunters than any of us, including you."

"You trust Caleb more than you do me."

I don't say anything, simply look at him. What is there to say? The truth is I don't trust him. He's given me more reasons to warrant my mistrust of him.

"Who are these hunters?" Doc finally asks after several awkward moments of silence.

"The guy I talked to was Cass Willow."

"I don't know him or his family personally, but I've heard good things about them."

"We need to get Wade and his crew's cameras out of the house. I don't want any of this to end up on their YouTube channel. It'll put Cass at risk too."

"I'm not sure if they caught anything on tape yesterday or not." Doc leans back in his chair. "I can take the cameras down today, but we need to worry about what they recorded last night."

Well, dang. I hadn't thought about that. I know we turned the cameras away before I did my thing, but they might have picked something up before then.

"I'll talk to Zeke. He should be able to fix it."

"Mattie…"

"Don't Mattie me, Doc. My dad isn't as bad as you think he is, and I'm betting he can fix this, even if it's with a bribe. He doesn't just kill people, you know."

Doc starts to say something but closes

his mouth instead. He shakes his head and turns back to the pages in front of him. Smart choice. "I've searched through everything I can find, but there is nothing here that might help us."

"I asked Zeke about it, and he's not sure what to do either. I threw Jonas in The Between, but that's not an option this time. She's stronger than he was, and there's no way the wraiths will get the jump on her. I'm hoping the hunters will be able to come up with something."

"If there was something we could find to remind her who she was, to make her remember her child, then we might stand a chance." Doc sighs and sits back.

Part of the reason I decided to major in psychology is so I can help the ghosts understand they're not only dead, but that they have to move on. Doc is right in that if we can find a way to reach her and ground her in who she was, we could get through to her. My psych degree will help me, but this is my first year of college, and I'm taking beginning courses. I don't have the tools I need yet.

And it's frustrating.

"Well, unless we can time travel back to before the fire, we have zero chance of finding something of Matilde's."

Doc snorts.

My sentiments exactly.

"At this point, I don't know what else to do. I hate to pin all our hopes on hunters who may or may not know how to deal with a soul eater."

"There's not much else to do, Doc. I think we need to go rest up and prepare for tonight. We both need sleep." I pause and glance toward the door, remembering the creeper out there. "They need to fix the lights down here."

"I'll walk you out. The ghost didn't bother me, so I'm guessing you're safe as long as I'm there."

"You gonna get some sleep?"

Doc starts packing his things. "Yes, but I want to check on Seth first."

"How is he?"

"He's in a coma the doctors can't explain."

"She took part of his soul." I hand Doc

his notebooks for him to pack into his briefcase. "It traumatized him in ways the doctors can't treat. He'll wake up when his soul is well enough, and not until."

This is something I know about all too well. Last year, when I smashed my own soul to kill Deleriel, I slept for weeks afterward. It was several days before I even opened my eyes. My dad gave me something to keep me awake long enough for Eli's funeral. Whatever potion he gave me was also a booster to my strength, and I was able to help carry his casket to his final resting place.

"Mattie?"

"Huh?" I blink at Doc's question. I must have zoned out.

"You okay?"

"Yeah, just old memories."

"Eli?"

I nod, not really wanting to talk about it anymore. There is something I should tell him, though, since he confessed his secret to me.

"I need to tell you something about Nathaniel."

He shuts his briefcase and looks around, making sure he hasn't left anything behind. "Hmm?"

"He's my brother."

Doc's gaze snaps back to me. "Your what?"

"He's Georgina's son. His grandparents, the Dubois, raised him."

The color slowly drains from Doc's face. His brown eyes, usually sharp and full of curiosity, dull. "Say again?"

"He came here to meet me." I fiddle with the button on my shirt, not wanting to meet his eyes, knowing they'll hold the same suspicion and fear Zeke's do. "I know better than to trust what he says, so you don't have to lecture me."

"Mattie, it's not that you can't trust him."

That gets my attention. "You're saying I can trust him?"

"No, of course not." He looks horrified at the very thought. "That came out wrong. What I meant is it's not only that you can't trust him. The Dubois family makes the Cranes look innocent. There's no telling what that boy is capable of."

"So far, he hasn't done anything, Doc, and he had a chance earlier today. He didn't try to steal my power while I was out. He carried me to safety. I'm not saying I trust him, because I don't, but I do want a chance to get to know him. He *is* my brother."

Doc starts pacing and muttering about foolishness under his breath.

"I don't want to worry you, but I thought you should know since he's Georgina's son."

"He's my nephew." The realization hits him like a punch straight to the gut. "Dear God. My nephew is a Dubois."

Well, he makes it sound like Nathaniel is the son of Satan. Wonder what that makes me.

"He's only here until his flight leaves tomorrow." I check my phone and see three missed texts from Dan. If I don't text him soon, he's going to start calling, or worse, he'll call Zeke.

"He's dangerous."

"I know that." I shoot off a quick text

to let him know I'm fine. "I'm not taking chances, honestly."

"I worry…"

"Not now, Doc. I'm still pissed at you."

"You're getting better at hiding it." He gives me a rueful look and picks up his briefcase. "Will you call me when you're not so angry?"

"I'll think about it."

"I can work with that." Doc smiles softly and escorts me out of the room and back to my car.

The creeper in the basement stayed away, and it makes me uneasy. He should have attacked Doc, but he didn't. I can't help but think back to that night I found out he was lying and the look in his eyes. It reminded me of the look Silas gets when he's doing something bad.

Could the ghost have stayed away from Doc because he was more scared of Doc than of me? And if that's the case, should I be more careful around Doc than I am even of Nathaniel?

The questions rattle around in my head

all the way home.

Sleep eludes me the rest of the day. I sit in my favorite spot in the garden and start to draw. The dream from last night won't leave me alone. I let it take over instead of focusing on Doc or Nathaniel. I need to unwind and let my mind wander where it would.

For the next several hours, I complete images of Matilde, of her in the kitchen, of her standing over the crib with a small smile on her face. I also draw the baby sleeping in his crib, as well as one of him in portrait style. I remember every single thing about him, and when I finally finish, even I'm amazed at the likeness to

249

not only the little boy, but his mother.

We couldn't find anything to remind Matilde of who she was because the fire destroyed everything that night, but maybe this will work. Maybe seeing images of herself and her little boy will be enough. It's better than nothing, and it's all I have.

Yawning, I stretch and get up. My hands are cramping. Funny how I never notice that until after I'm done. While I'm drawing, my fingers are like the river, flowing and never-ending. It's something that has always struck me as odd, but most artists are like that. At least the ones I've paid attention to.

Zeke is in his office, per usual, looking stressed. "Still haven't found the shipment?"

"Oh, we found it, but another village that's in desperate straits captured it. I can't very well take it from them. I'm organizing a new shipment instead."

"That's nice of you." I flop down on the couch. "I think I might have an in with the ghost."

"Really?" Zeke stops staring at his computer screen and turns his attention to me. "What did you come up with?"

I flip open my sketchpad and show him the drawings I did earlier in the garden. "I'm hoping these will spark some kind of memory in her."

"These are beautiful, *ma petite*." He stands to take a closer look at the sketches. "I still say you should have majored in art."

"Eh, it's something I'm already good at. I'm hoping by getting a degree in psychology, it'll help me with the ghosts and dealing with the people in your business if I should have to. Being able to read people is always a bonus."

Zeke smiles, but it doesn't quite reach his eyes. Something's bothering him, but he's not going to tell me. I'm guessing it has to do with Nathaniel. It's not anything he's said or done; it's more of a feeling. The more time I spend with Zeke, the closer we become and the more in tune we are with each other. Even with my mom, I never shared this kind of connection. I'm grateful for it, though.

"If only I thought you'd take to the boardroom like you do a ghost hunt." He hands the sketchpad back to me.

"Yeah…no. Sorry, Papa."

This time his smile is genuine, if a little rueful. "Mrs. Jones is preparing an early dinner for you all. She thought you might want to go into your adventure on a full stomach."

My stomach growls in response. Mrs. Jones is the best cook ever.

Zeke laughs. "There's my girl."

Hey, my stomach has a mind and a voice of its own. I can't control it.

"Are Mary and Eric up yet?"

"Last I checked, no. Nathaniel left about an hour before you woke up. He wanted to go back to his hotel, and I had a driver take him."

"You didn't tell me." We'd had a long talk about Nathaniel, and he didn't think to tell me he'd already left?

He doesn't quite meet my eyes, which means Nathaniel was probably asked to leave. Zeke wouldn't want him near me if he could help it.

"*Papa*."

"I'm not apologizing." His stark blue eyes are lit with fire and determination. "He's lying to us. I don't know how, but he's managing it. I don't want him near you until I can figure out what he's up to."

"We talked about this."

"You talked. I never agreed." His tone hardens. "I will keep you safe, *ma petite*, even if that means protecting you from yourself."

Speaking of keeping me safe…

"Uh, I had a talk with Doc earlier, and I think you need to know about it."

"Doc?"

"Dr. Olivet."

"Ah, the Spook Doctor."

Doc hates that nickname, but it's stuck. It's what everyone calls him, thanks to the internet memes.

"Come sit down." I pat the seat beside me, and Zeke's instantly on alert. "This is gonna take a while."

For the next hour, I go over everything

I learned about Doc and my mom and even my reaction to learning the truth. Zeke stays quiet through most of it, only asking a question here or there until I'm finished.

When I'm done, we sit there in silence. As the minutes tick by and still no response from my father, alarms start to go off. I'm scary when I'm angry, but Zeke is downright terrifying. His silence is a surefire tell. He's pissed.

"He knew who you were all along?"

Oh, yeah, my dad is mad.

"He thought he was protecting me."

"I would never harm a hair on your head."

"I know that, Papa, but he could only go by what Claire told him. To him, you were the biggest threat to me."

"All that time you spent in foster care when you could have been here with me, safe. Everything that happened to you, Eli, your sister, and Daniel could have been prevented if he'd only said something."

"That's one way of looking at it."

He growls. Literally growls. "How else do you see it?"

"Before I met Dan, I didn't know how to love people or to let them love me. Foster care doesn't teach you that. You get shuffled from home to home with mostly apathetic people who only see you as a monthly check. Don't get me wrong, there are good homes out there. I was in a few, but I always wrecked them because I was afraid. Afraid they'd reject me. Then there were the bad ones. Those stick with you. You never get past it. Those homes shape you. They teach you to hit first and ask questions later just to survive."

"Sweetheart…"

"No." I hold up my hand to stop him. "I need you to listen. You need to really understand this, Papa."

He nods, and I continue.

"Dan was the first person who never gave up on me, no matter how hard I pushed him away. He showed me it was possible to love someone, and he showed me I was worth letting someone love me. Then there's Mary. She taught me what family was all about. Her and her mom. They took me in and loved me for me, even knowing I could see ghosts, and those things could follow me home. They didn't care. They loved me anyway and became my family."

I push up off the couch and start to pace, trying to find the words I need. It's not easy confessing all this. I may not trust Doc, but at the same time, I want Zeke to understand that if he'd come into my life sooner, we might be sitting at a far different outcome than we are today.

"The things I suffered at the hands of Mrs. Olsen, Jonas, and all the ghost girls trying to murder me made me stronger, not because of the experience itself, but because I had people to fight for, people who mattered to me, people I mattered to. They gave me something to live for."

"I know that, *ma petite*."

"Do you, though? Had Doc told me about you, then Dan and I wouldn't have gotten as close as we did. I would never have moved into the Crosses'. Love would have been a foreign concept to me.

You would have tried, but I wouldn't have been ready to let you love me or to let myself love you. And I would have had no one who mattered enough for me to fight tooth and nail for. I would have died, Papa. I might not even have taken Deleriel out with me either. He could be out there now, terrorizing and feeding off little kids. I wouldn't change anything that happened to me. Those things made me the person I am, gave me something to fight for, and in the end, saved my life. That's how I look at it."

He says nothing for several moments, simply staring at me. I can't tell what he's thinking, as his face is as blank as an empty sheet of drawing paper.

Finally, he gets up and hugs me so tight I can't breathe. "You are an exceptional young woman, Emma Rose Mathilda Hathaway Crane."

He very rarely uses the name my mother gave me, even if he allowed it to be put on my birth certificate. He hates her for taking me from him, but he's stopped hating on her in front of me, at least. She's the reason I'm standing here. If she hadn't come to me after I smashed my soul, I might be dead now. He knows that, and it's put him in her debt, something he despises, but is grateful for nonetheless.

"Thank you," I whisper and hug him back.

"Yo, Hathaway!"

"Eric's up." I laugh and pull away from Zeke. "Which means Mary's up, and we need to eat before we head over to the Duchaines'."

"Want me to come with you?" Zeke asks.

"No, you don't have a protection tattoo against Miss Piggy."

"Protection tattoo?"

"Silas gave it to me earlier."

Zeke's nostrils flare. "That demon needs to keep his distance."

"He's only protecting me, same as you."

Zeke's lips thin, but he can't argue with that.

"Hathaway, where you at, girl?"

"Coming!" I call. "Come on, Papa, let's go eat. I'm sure Mrs. Jones will appreciate an early evening."

With that, Zeke follows me into the kitchen. I'm still not sure what he's going to say to Doc when he sees him, but I hope I got through enough that he doesn't put a hit out on the man.

We'll see.

The drive back to the Duchaines' later that evening is subdued. Eric and Mary are both worried it's too much for me. The headache worried them both, but I'm still sure it was just a stress headache. I'm not about to do anything to cause my death if I can help it, which means the first hint that the headache is something more, I'll be the first person to volunteer myself to go to the emergency room.

I told them about Doc over dinner. Eric agrees with Zeke, and Mary is on the cautious side, more of a Dan reaction, as I call it. A wait and see kind of thing. I still don't know how I feel about the situation. On one side, he lied to me yet again, and on the other, he's done nothing but help me.

But there's something there, something that creeps me out. I can't shake the memory of that night and how he'd looked at me. Maybe I'm reading too much into it, but I can't let myself fully trust him.

I may never.

The Scooby Gang is parked in the driveway, along with a black convertible. Nathaniel is sitting in the driver's seat talking on his phone. When he sees us pull up, he says something then hangs up. A small smile is tossed our way, and Mary glares. She doesn't trust my brother any more than I trust Doc.

It's the old, beat-up Ford Mustang parked in front of the house that has my attention. I pull in behind it, curious. It's not the kind of car you'd typically see in this neighborhood. This is a middle-class neighborhood where everyone drives sedans and mini-vans.

Two guys and a girl pile out of the

Mustang as soon as I shut off the engine of my car. They all look alike, so I'm assuming they're family, with their dirty blond hair and brown eyes. None of them is older than twenty-five, and the girl looks to be about sixteen. It makes my heart clench for a minute, thinking of Ava, Eli, and Caleb.

Pushing aside those depression-inducing thoughts, I get out of the car and go to meet them. "One of you guys Cass?"

"Me." The tallest of the guys steps forward. He towers over my five-foot, three-inch frame. "You Mattie Hathaway?"

"No one calls me that anymore. I'm Emma Crane."

His eyes narrow. Crane is a well-known name here in the south. "Any relation to Ezekiel Crane?"

"He's my dad."

The other two start muttering, and he shoots them a look that says *shut it*. "We didn't know that."

"Who my dad is doesn't change the

fact we have a ghost inside who's trying to murder the little girl who lives here. I want it gone and will do what I can, with or without your help."

"Caleb vouched for you. Said you were good people. He never mentioned you were a Crane."

"I didn't know I was a Crane until about a year ago. I grew up in foster care."

"Huh," the girl huffs.

"Look, if this is a problem for you, I get it, but before you bounce, can you at least tell me if you found a way to get rid of the ghost?"

"We were gonna wing it." He gives me a mischievous grin, reminding me so much of Eli, my heart cracks a little.

"Winging it almost got us all killed yesterday," Nathaniel says, coming to stand beside me.

"Cass Willow, this is my brother, Nathaniel Buchard."

A slow hiss escapes Cass. "A Crane and a Dubois. What is Caleb getting us into here?"

"Yes, yes, we're all very bad people." Nathaniel flicks his hand. "Doesn't change the fact we need to work together to help the people who live here."

"Why would you want to help?" Cass asks.

"Because she does. I don't really care what happens here one way or another, but I'm not about to let my sister go and get herself killed just because she has a misguided sense of responsibility and a need to help people."

Well, I wasn't expecting that to come out of my brother's mouth.

"I am who I am, Emma." He gives me a small, tight smile. "I wasn't raised to care about anyone outside of my family. These people don't matter to me, but you do."

Mary's outraged gasp more than sums up all our feelings.

"Okay, now that we've had our Dr. Phil moment, can we get on with this?" Eric drawls. "We all got class on Monday, and I don't want to spend all day tomorrow here."

"We still have the Scooby Gang's cameras to deal with." I nod toward the van. I'm guessing the guys are inside, having beaten us here to make sure their equipment is running properly.

"Taken care of, *cher*." Cass flashes me a grin. "Robert is going to send out a little EMP bomb that'll fry their equipment."

"Won't that fry the electronics in our cars too, though?" Mary moves closer, trying to get a look at what Robert is carrying.

"Naw, *cher*. We'll let it off inside, and it has a maximum range of a few feet. Our cars are safe."

"I'm Caryle, Cass's cousin, and this is my brother Robert." Caryle sticks her hand out, and I shake it automatically. Seems some of my grandmother's subtle lessons on manners are working. "Never worked with the enemy before."

"I'm not the enemy."

"That has yet to be seen." Robert finally speaks up. His voice is rough and deeper. It sounds more like it should be

265

coming out of the mouth of someone much older.

Doc pulls up, cutting off whatever we're about to say. He gets out and gives us his best curious expression. "Doc, come meet the hunters Caleb sent us." I motion him over.

"Who this be, *cher*?"

"Dr. Lawrence Olivet."

"You know the Spook Doctor?" Caryle sounds impressed.

"Don't call him that," I whisper. "He hates it."

They all three nod then greet him when I introduce everyone.

"Well, seems we have a full house." Doc's gaze skirts to Nathaniel and then away. I haven't had a chance to tell Nathaniel who Doc is yet, but I'm not doing it around all these strangers.

"You guys gonna hang out there on the sidewalk all night?" Ethan calls from the front porch. Eric perks up at the sound of his voice, and Mary gets a knowing smile on her face. I shake my head at her, and her smile wilts. I don't want her to embarrass him. It's hard enough dealing with the feelings he's having without her adding to it.

"I didn't think they'd be here this early," Doc muses as we file up the steps and into the house.

"Wade wants answers. If I were in his shoes, I'd be here early too." Too bad he's not going to get his answers tonight.

Wade is waiting in the living room where all the computer monitors are set up. Like I expected, he wants answers. It's clear in the sharpness of his stare.

"Fancy." Caryle whistles.

"Who are all these people?" Wade asks suspiciously.

"Colleagues of mine," Doc answers and sets his briefcase down on the table. "Is that a problem?"

"Of course not." Wade is such a suck-up when it comes to Doc.

"With Seth out of commission, I needed backup." Doc turns around, his gaze sweeping over us. "This has gotten very dangerous."

"How's your assistant?" Ethan asks,

the only one of the Scooby Gang who seems to have good manners.

"Not well. I'm going to have to start giving that boy hazard pay."

Wade moves to the front of his little group. "About that, we have some questions."

"No time for questions right now." Doc brushes his attempted inquiry aside. "We have to talk about the ghost. We've identified the type of ghost it is, and I think it's too dangerous for everyone to be in the house tonight."

"Type of ghost?" Jordan asks. I'd forgotten the little guy was there buried in the computer monitors. He hardly ever speaks, at least in the time we've been around him. "I didn't know there were different kinds."

"Oh, yes." Doc nods sagely. "There are many different kinds. This particular one feeds off the souls of the living until there's nothing left. It's what happened to Seth. His body went into shock when a part of his soul went missing."

"She likes the way little kids tastes,

268

specifically," I clarify. "Her name is Matilde Hernandez. She and her infant son died in the fire of 1922."

"No one died in that fire." Wade shook his head. "We checked."

"You didn't check the Historical Society," Doc chastises in his critical tone. "The library lost a lot of records in Katrina, but the HS moved their sensitive documents out before the hurricane hit."

Wade blushes. No one likes to be made a fool of in front of their idol.

"We are not sure how to remove her, though." This time it's Doc's turn to be unsure. "I've been scouring through research all day and have made inquiries into the community, but we are all at a loss."

"I have something that may help." I hand him the sketches I've been clutching since I got out of the car. "These are what she and her son looked like. I'm hoping we'll be able to get through to her with them."

"How do you know what they look like?" Wade's expression is calculating.

269

"I'm a little psychic," I lie. "I picked up on it yesterday and just drew what I saw."

Wade pushes through Mary and Eric to get to Doc, who's going through the drawings.

"These are excellent, Emma. They definitely can't hurt." Doc hands the drawings back to me, ignoring Wade's attempt to get a better look.

"May I?" Cass asks, and I hand him the drawings. He lets out a whistle. "Where'd you learn to draw like this?"

I shrug. "I've always been able to."

"*Magnifique*," Cass says and hands them back to me.

"Thank you."

"I don't want everyone in the house while we deal with the ghost. It will be too hard to keep everyone safe spread out. I want only a few of us in here while we exorcise this ghost."

Doc's words drop like a bomb, and Wade's face screws up. "I have every right to be here. Mr. Duchaine agreed we could film this for our channel."

"Your safety trumps your channel, *mon amie*." Cass walks over and throws an arm around Wade. "We can't have you dying on film, now, can we?"

Wade shrugs him off and scoots several feet away. Cass winks at him, causing both Eric and Ethan to laugh. They look at each other, and you can't miss the blush on either of their faces. It's cute, and Mary's smart enough to keep her mouth shut this time.

"And you're an expert?" Wade grouches.

"*Oui, cher*. We are the ones who get called in when a ghost goes rogue. Can you say you've ever faced down a deranged ghost and lived to tell the tale?"

"We've been in plenty of situations…"

"I'm sure you've been in 'haunted houses' before, but I guarantee you've never faced a soul eater."

Cass's words shut Wade up, but I know he's not done arguing. If all else fails, he'll sneak in and see what's going on.

The computer monitors go dead, and

Jordan lets out a noise somewhere between a whine and a cry of alarm. "What the…"

"What happened?" Wade frowns and runs over to his screens.

"I don't know. It all just died." Jordan leans down and makes sure nothing came unplugged.

Robert winks at me.

Poor Jordan. He's going to be trying to figure that one out for a while.

"Hey, my camera's dead too." Nathan takes it off his shoulder and starts inspecting it. "I put fresh batteries in this thing right before we came inside."

"What did you do?" Wade's hostile gaze centers on me.

"Me?" I look around, the most innocent expression I can muster on my face. "How could I do anything to your computers? I'm standing way over here. I haven't gone near them."

I'm starting to get the feeling good old Wade doesn't like me.

"I don't know what you did, but I know you did something."

"Chill, man." Ethan puts his camera on the coffee table. "It's a setback, but we'll deal with it. We can use the smaller camcorders in the van. It'll all be good."

No, it won't, but I'm not saying that one out loud.

"So, what do you want to do?" I ask Doc when Ethan and Wade go to look for more cameras.

"They'll be vulnerable, and we can't take that chance. We need them out of the house."

"Call the Duchaines," I suggest. "If they tell them to get out, they'll have to."

"I should have thought about that," Doc mutters and pulls out his phone. He steps away to make his call.

"They are annoying, especially that one arguing." Caryle flops down on the couch, ignoring Jordan's gasp of outrage.

"They're the Scooby Gang," I tell her and crack a smile.

"Ohmygosh!" she rushes out all at once, her face lighting up with her laughter. "That so fits."

"We are not the Scooby Gang," Jordan

tells us both, trying and failing to look tough. A guy with curly red hair just can't look tough. Caryle and I both break down in a fit of laughter. I think I'm gonna like this girl.

Wade storms back in the house a few minutes later, livid and shouting about how we ruined his show. Big deal. I wouldn't care at all if it weren't for Mary. She looks ready to cry because he's throwing daggers at her with his eyes.

"I'm not throwing you off the property, just out of the house while I work." Doc doesn't look the least bit apologetic. "You are more than welcome to interview me afterward, but I can't risk your safety. I'm not letting Eric or Mary in the house while we do this either."

Much to their credit, neither say a word, which further calms Wade. At the mention of an interview with the renowned parapsychologist, Wade deflates like a sad balloon after a four-year-old's birthday party.

"Now, if you'll all move this party outside, we can get to work." Robert opens the front door and waits until everyone is outside except for me, Nathaniel, Doc, and the Willows.

Time to work.

Robert and Caryle go to make sure none of the cameras will capture us as we work. I'm a little hesitant letting them go by themselves, but then I remind myself they're hunters. They can probably handle themselves better than anyone else.

Doesn't mean I can shake the worry from my mind after what happened to me and Seth. This ghost is dangerous.

Cass throws a duffle bag on the kitchen table. Where did that come from? I don't remember him carrying it before, but one of the others may have had it, and I just didn't notice.

He pulls out a shotgun and several knives.

"Why do you need a gun?" I ask, curious. It would be the last thing I'd think to bring.

"Shells are filled with rock salt, *cher*." Cass loads the gun then sets it on the table. "It will make the ghost scatter."

Another memory hits me of the last ghost hunt I went on in New Orleans when I first met the Malones. They'd used a shotgun to make the demon trying to kill me scatter to the wind. I'll have to look into getting one and keeping it in the car. Which means I need a permit. Might not go over so well if they can get access to my juvie record.

"You don't have a hunter's kit, *cher*?" Cass looks up from inventorying the weapons in his bag.

"I'm not a hunter."

He cocks his head and stares. "Caleb made it sound like you were."

"I'm not. I try to stay as far away from using my gifts as I can. Nobody wants to be a freak show."

"Then how are you involved in this?" He raises a brow in question.

"It's a long story, and one we don't have time for now." I hear Caryle and Robert coming back down the hall. "Now that I'm here, the only thing I want to do is help."

"We're all clear." Caryle bounces in the room, her dirty blonde pigtails flying behind her. "I think our ghost is here. The whole place feels off, especially the nursery."

"She's been feeding off the baby." Doc closes his laptop. "She also attacked Ma…Emma and Seth in there. She's attached to that room."

"Probably because it's a nursery. The whole reason she's so pissed is because they murdered her baby. It makes sense she'd feel stronger and more at ease in a nursery."

"Bad mojo," Robert mutters. "Little kids should be off limits to everyone, living and dead."

He and Cass pound each other's fist in agreement. Caryle rolls her eyes at their

278

antics. One thing I've noticed is that guys will be guys, no matter how old they are.

"So, what's the game plan?" I ask, steering everyone's attention back to the task at hand. "Any ideas of how to take her down?"

"We don't have our blessed blade, but we do have iron."

"That's only going to piss her off." I've seen her pissed off, and it's not pretty. "Let me try to get through to her first, to make her remember who she was."

"With those pictures of yours?" Cass nods to the drawings I'm still holding. "Not sure she's gonna give you time to talk, *cher*."

"The Cajun could be right." Nathaniel pushes off the wall to come join the group. I'd almost forgotten he was here, he was being so quiet. "Especially after what you did to her yesterday."

"What did you do?" Caryle looked curious.

I don't know if I should say anything. I'm not one for telling strangers about my abilities.

"She trapped the ghost in a circle of The Between and then defused her when she started eating souls from in there."

That got their attention, and I shoot my brother a look that says he's toast later.

He merely shrugs. "Don't hide who you are, Emma. You're special, and you shouldn't be ashamed of that."

"How did you do that?" Cass asks, clearly intrigued.

"I'm a living reaper. I can see ghosts even when others can't, the good ones and the bad ones. Hunters usually only see the ones that have gone bad. They're as real to me as all of you standing here."

"Really?" Caryle squeals. "I've read about living reapers, but I've never met one before."

"I don't advertise it."

"You should," Cass says. "Nathaniel is right. That's a rare gift, and it can help so many people. Not just living people, but ghosts too. They deserve to move on, to not be trapped here. Why would you hide that away, *cher*?"

"Because I don't want to be a freak." I turn away from them all. "I came to New Orleans to get away from that part of me. I don't want to be known as the weird girl."

"You're not weird, *cher*, not to us." Cass takes my arm and pulls me around. "You're a freaking legend come to life for hunters. Your gift would help us more than you could ever imagine. You could save lives. I can't tell you how many hunters die because they can't see what you do. Isn't that as important as being normal? Maybe even more so?"

He's like Dan and Eli all rolled into one. He makes sense, but there's an element of devilry in him.

"Can we talk about this later?" I am not up for this conversation. "I want to get this ghost gone."

"Of course, darlin'." Cass winks, and I know this conversation isn't over. He's like a dog with a bone. He's gonna try to wear me down until I give in.

"Let me try first. Nathaniel, you're with me. I want everyone else outside the door in case we need help." I don't wait for an agreement, and head toward the staircase with Nathaniel on my heels.

The nursery is just as I remembered it, very girly and cold. It's not quite as cold as it could be, but the ghost is here. I can feel her watching us from the shadows. She's pissed. It's not hard to feel all that anger pulsing from the very walls. I close the door behind us and walk to the center of the room.

"Matilde, I know you're in here."

There's a shift in the air. My knowing her name surprised her.

"That's right," I say and spin slowly in a circle, looking for the slightest abnormality in the shadows. "I know what happened to you and your little boy. I'm sorry about that."

The temperature in the room takes a nosedive. She's listening.

"Do you want to see your little boy again? I can help you do that if you let me."

The anger ratchets up another notch. Nathaniel shifts closer to me. "I don't think this is working. It seems to only be pissing her off more."

I agree, but I still have to try.

"Do you remember this?" I hold up the drawing of her and slowly turn, making sure she can see it wherever she's hiding. "Or this one?" I do the same turn, this time of her standing over a baby's bassinet. "It's you and your little boy."

That gets her attention. A blast of cold air hits us so hard, we both stagger back under its weight. Toys are picked up and thrown at us, hitting us and the wall in the process. A wooden block catches me on the forehead, and a small trickle of blood flows from the wound, leaking onto the paper I'm holding.

The sharp intake of breath from Nathaniel tells me that one drop of blood did what I never wanted anyone to find out I could do. My blood brings images to life. Glancing down, I see the image shift and move, the woman bending down and tucking the little one into bed.

While Nathaniel might have seen it, Miss Piggy either didn't or simply ignored it. She's coming at us again, this time with furniture.

"Emma, you okay in there?" Caryle shouts.

"We're fine!"

"No, we're not!" Nathaniel yells at the door. "This crazy ghost has gone psycho!"

I glare at him. "I'm the reaper here, not you. Sometimes it takes time to get through to them." I dodge the rocking chair, but barely. Dang, this ghost is pissy. "Don't come in here, Caryle!"

I can hear either Cass or Robert cussing so loud it comes through all the noise in here. She's furious. Furniture, toys, books, they're all flying through the air with the sole purpose of harming us.

"Why am I in here with you, then?" Nathaniel asks. "If you don't want my help…"

"You're in here with me because you're my brother." A flying clown slams Nathaniel in the chest, and he freaks out. Like, starts screaming, freaking out. He flings the thing so far across the room, I'd be dying laughing if we weren't in danger.

"You're afraid of clowns?"

"You're not?" Nathaniel shudders. "They're creepy."

Silence.

Everything falls to the floor around us, and we're left with eerie silence. Even the temperature spikes upward.

She's gone.

"Where did she go?" Nathaniel whispers.

"I don't know, but she's not here."

Well, this sucks.

I open the bedroom door, and everyone stares in at the complete mess. "You get her?" Robert asks.

"No. She just left. Now we have to go track her down."

"And then what?"

No one answers because no one has a clue.

We split into pairs, this time Nathaniel going off with Doc, and Cass with me. Doc asked for Nathaniel to go with him, and I guess maybe he wants a chance to get to know him, same as me. I shake my head slightly at Doc to let him know I haven't told Nathaniel about him, and he nods in understanding before they head off to check the living areas. Robert and Caryle take the other bedrooms, leaving me and Cass with the basement.

My favorite spot in any house…not.

Cass leads the way down the steps. At least it's bright down here. They must have hundred-watt bulbs or something.

286

The basement itself isn't scary. It's not finished, per se, but there is sheetrock up on the walls, and we can see a layout for a bathroom roughed in in the far corner. I'm grateful it's not all dark crevices and exposed dirt or crappy brick that's Lord only knows how old.

It does smell, though. It's what a haunted basement would smell like—rot and decay. It reminds me of the scent earlier at the library, tinged with anger and putrid hatred.

"This is a bad place, *cher*." Cass stands beside me, surveying the open space around us. "She's here."

"Yeah, I know." I wrap my arms around myself, the drawing clutched tightly in one hand. "I don't think there's much we can do to get through to her."

"Sometimes there's no saving them."

And that's the God's truth.

We move deeper into the underground lair. "The first time we saw her, she sank through the floor under the rocking chair." Glancing up, I make a guesstimate as to where Hailey's nursery would be.

"There." I point to the east corner. "That's where she would have come from."

"They been remodeling?" Cass moves toward the corner of the basement, his shotgun up and at the ready.

"Yeah. The owners inherited the house and did a complete remodel. We think that's what started this whole mess."

"That'll do it." Cass stops a few feet from where we assume the ghost resides. This corner is darker, and there seems to be some water damage on the new sheetrock. The floor is warped, the same water damage as the walls.

The temperature has slowly been dropping since we descended the stairs. I noticed it right away, and I'm assuming Cass did as well. It's so cold we can see our breath every time we exhale.

There's a creaking noise, and the pipes in the roughed-in bathroom area start to shake, small droplets of water leaking out from between where the pipes connect to each other.

"That's not good," I whisper and take a

step backward.

"No, it's not." Cass turns, and his eyes widen two seconds before I realize Miss Piggy is behind me. Before I can move, she latches on. She lets out a savage scream when she realizes she can't feed off me. You'd think she would have learned that lesson yesterday.

I yank myself away, and Cass shouts for me to duck. I fall flat and roll just as the shotgun blasts above me. Another unearthly scream bounces around the basement. I look up to see Cass shoot again, but it has no effect on the ghost. She advances with a determination I've only ever seen once. When Jonas came after me.

I'm on my feet and pull out my little pocketknife. I spring the blade and slash at her. She turns from Cass to snarl at me. There is nothing but murder in her eyes. She's going to do what she can to make sure I never get up again.

This time when her hands grip me, she's not trying to feed. Instead, her cold seeps inside me, and her hands wrap around my heart and start to squeeze. I may be soul-proof, but I'm not infallible.

It infuriates me, and the reaper that lives inside me comes out, wrapping my own power around her, and we tangle together, neither willing to give an inch. Cass is shouting, and I hear more footsteps pound down the stairs, undoubtedly drawn by the shotgun blasts.

But I can't focus on any of that, only on the ghost trying to stop my heart.

Cass puts the shotgun right against her temple and fires. Rock salt goes everywhere, and she lets loose long enough for me to get away, but she's still bound to me because I have my tentacles into *her*.

"Let her go, Emma." Nathaniel is right behind me. "You can't force her to cross over, and you can't throw her into The Between. You told me that yourself. We need to regroup and figure out another way."

I have a better idea.

She can't get away as long as I have hold of her. I take out the last picture I haven't shown her, the portrait of her son. I hold it up to her, and she has nowhere to go, nowhere to hide. She's forced to look at it.

Once she does, some of the fight goes out of her, and she stops struggling so hard. "Do you see, Matilde? It's your son. I can help you see him again."

The wave of shame that rolls off her is so intense, I almost lose my grasp on her. Why is she ashamed?

"Matilde?"

She looks at me, and some of the white leaves her face, the black streaks melting away until it resembles a human face.

"What happened that night?"

"It was my fault."

"What was your fault?" I ask, switching to an internal dialogue only she and I can hear.

"The fire." A tear rolls out of her eye and down her cheek. *"My son died because of me."*

"Matilde, you were injured. You couldn't save him."

"I tried to go to him, but I stumbled,

and the candle rolled off the table. The curtains caught fire, and it spread so fast."

"Honey, the fire didn't kill him. It was the man who went up the stairs. The fire only hid the true cause of your deaths. He was gone before the fire ever touched him."

A low sob escapes her, and she reaches for the drawing. I let her have it. I'm shocked she has enough energy left to hold it. I would have thought the fight she put up would have drained her.

The longer she looks at the sketch, the more the real her emerges, until a young Hispanic woman is standing there, holding the photo to her chest and crying.

"Matilde, you can't keep punishing others and stealing the lives of children because your son is gone."

"They deserve it," she says. *"They came for us, not caring that my little one was innocent."*

"Mrs. Harcourt did, but not all the innocents you attacked. You can't keep doing that. It's time for you to go, to be with your son."

All the anger that started to fill up her expression falters. *"See my Henry again?"*

"Yes," I tell her solemnly. "Do you want to see him?"

She nods. *"How?"*

I look to the opposite wall and focus on every happy thought I have, and within a few seconds, a door opens, the light so bright it hurts the eyes. "All you have to do is go into that light. Henry will be waiting for you."

"I..." She squints, and a look of wonder comes over her face. *"Mama?"*

"Is your mother waiting for you?" I know it's a reaper in the form of a loved one, but I won't burst her bubble.

"Yes, she's calling to me. She says Henry misses me."

"Then go to her, Matilde. Go into the light and be with your family." I let go of her, so there's nothing tethering her to this place. "It's okay, Matilde, go."

"The things I've done because of my pain..." She trails off, and her expression

becomes fearful. *"How will I be judged?"*

"God forgives, Matilde, but we answer for all the things we do in this life. I can't say it'll be all roses, but I do know there is nothing but love in that light, and your family is there. That's what you need to focus on, how much you love them and how it'll feel to hold your son again."

There is still guilt and shame within her, but her resistance fades, and a sad smile tilts her lips. *"I will go and be judged for all the pain I caused here, but then I will see my son, and whatever atonement I must make will be worth it to hold my Henry again."*

"Then, go." I sweep my hand toward the light. "Go and be at peace."

"Thank you for helping me, even when I tried to hurt you."

"This is what I do. It's my job to help you."

She nods and turns toward the light. She takes a hesitant step and then another until she's running toward her mother and the hope of seeing her son once more.

The light fades, and warmth floods the room, a clear indicator that our ghost has crossed over.

"Shiiii—"

I put a finger against Cass's lips. "No cussing."

"She doesn't cuss," Doc tells them. "Be respectful of that around her."

They're all staring at me with a myriad of emotions. This is why I don't tell people what I can do, let alone allow them to see me do it. I'm a freak. I know it, but I'd hoped to never have anyone look at me like that again.

I turn and go up the stairs, intent on getting away from all of it, and run smack into a hard chest. Looking up, puppy dog brown eyes are staring down at me, a smile tilting his lips.

"Dan!" I fling my arms around him and hug him so tight, I think I might have cut off his circulation. "What are you doing here?"

"I heard you might have been in need of a blessed blade, but you seem to have handled it all on your own."

He lifts me up, and I wrap my legs around him and hold on while he backs up out of the kitchen and carries me into the living room, sitting on the couch and holding onto me as tightly as I am him.

"I know you said you wanted to do this on your own, to be you without me, but what if I can't be me without *you*? Ever think of that?"

I bury my head between his neck and shoulder, breathing in the unique scent that is all Dan. He never wears aftershave. His scent is clean and tinged slightly with the soap he uses, and I love it. I've missed it, missed him so much.

Doc clears his throat, and I hear Dan greet him, but I keep my head buried. I'm not ready to face everyone yet and how they look at me.

"We'll be outside," Doc says. "Take your time. No one's going anywhere."

"Thanks." Dan's hands tighten around me, and I listen as they all file outside and the front door closes. "You okay, Squirt?"

"No," I whisper, "but I'm better now that you're here. I missed you."

He tilts my head up so he can see me. "I missed you too." Then he leans down and kisses me, a kiss so soft and sweet it melts every bone in my body.

"I thought you were working." I lean back once he lets my lips have some relief.

"I am, but when Caleb told me what was going on, and you told him not to come, I couldn't sit there and do nothing. You needed me. It was that simple, so I came."

"I'm glad you ignored me." He respects my boundaries, but when it comes to my safety, I don't think there's anything he won't do to protect me. Even ignore me when I tell him to stay away.

"Me too." He kisses my temple and hugs me to him. "As soon as Mom's trial is over, I'm going to put in my resumé with the police department down here. Being away from you, especially when I know you're in danger, it's too hard, Mattie."

"Emma."

He snorts, and I laugh. He will never call me Emma.

"You're Mattie to me, and you always will be."

"Can I ask you something?"

"Sure, baby, ask away."

Oh-Em-Gee! He called me baby. It slipped off his tongue as naturally as breathing. My chest swells.

"What you told Nathaniel earlier on the phone, about me being your girlfriend…"

"Yeah?"

"Were you just saying that so he'd know I have someone besides Zeke looking out for me, or…"

"Or did I mean it?" He finishes the question for me.

I nod, keeping my head against his chest where I can feel how rapidly his heart is beating. That's a good sign, right?

"When I met you, I knew you were special. I felt this tug I'd never felt around anyone, and at first, I tried to tell myself it was just because you had no one and you were like a little sister to me. I tried to keep you firmly in the sister zone. I tried, and I managed it for a long time." He lets out a heavy sigh before continuing. "Then I got to know Meg. I loved her, and her passing hurt, but it made me realize something."

"What?" I ask softly.

"That I'd rather lose anyone as long as it wasn't you. The thought of losing you cripples me, Mattie Louise Hathaway."

"So, you haven't met anyone while we've been apart?"

"Oh, I've met plenty of girls, even thought about asking out a few."

I freeze. Officer Dan went out with another girl? I'm gonna murder him.

"But when I walked up to one to try, I couldn't do it. They weren't you. You're it for me, Squirt. I can wait for you as long as you need me to, but you're mine, and I'm gonna marry you one day."

Tears flood my eyes, and I let them fall. After everything that happened today, after all the stares and the looks from the Willow crew, hearing Dan say this is just too much.

"Hey, now, what's with the waterworks?" The alarm in his voice is comical, but I only cry harder.

"I'm sorry, I just…"

"Shh, baby. It's okay. I didn't mean to make you cry."

I'm not sure how long we sit there before my tears stop and I'm able to talk again. He still didn't answer my question, though. "Does that mean you weren't just calling me your girlfriend to protect me from my brother?"

He laughs low, and it sends shivers racing up and down my spine. "You're mine, Squirt. No one else is ever laying their lips on you again."

"No more thinking about asking other girls out either." The words come out dark and harsh, my jealousy rearing its ugly head.

"Hey, look at me."

When I do, he blinks. "Your eyes are black."

"I…I can't control it. It's part of me."

"Hey. Don't look at me like that."

"Like what?"

"Like you expect me to be disgusted and walk away. I know you're part demon. I know that part comes to life when you feel threatened or someone you love is threatened. It woke up when you thought I was dead. You used that part of yourself to protect me."

"I wasn't going to let you die."

He gives me another of those half smiles that make a girl melt. "Remember what I told you about you and me?"

"That you're in for the long haul?"

"Half-demon and all." He kisses the tip of my nose. "There isn't a part of you I don't love. There's nothing you will ever do or say to chase me away. Make me mad as hell, sure, but I won't ever walk away from you. You're mine, and I keep what's mine."

"You've gotten very possessive since I last saw you." He's more intense too, more...everything.

"I just know what I want, and that happens to be you. I know you wanted me to stay away so you could prove to yourself you can be strong without me. I'm not going to interfere with that, but I want to be here for you, for when you do need me."

"I proved all that to myself today. I was able to solve my own mess without any help from you. I am a strong woman, but that doesn't mean I can't make room for you. I want you here, Dan. I know it's selfish because your entire family is in Charlotte, but I can't live there."

"I know, baby. Too many bad memories, but I can't be there without you either. You're stuck with me as soon as the trial's over."

"It starts next month?"

He nods, and some of the happiness leaves his eyes.

"I'll be there."

"Promise?"

"Promise, Officer Dan."

"Come on, Squirt. Let's go outside before Mary decides to barge in. I think she's at her limit."

I laugh just thinking about her. She probably is ready to burst through the doors. I scramble off Dan's lap, and he stands and pulls me to him, keeping an arm around me as we go outside into the night.

Dan steers us right toward Nathaniel, who's leaning against his car. Dan sticks his hand out, and Nathaniel shakes it automatically. "I'm Dan."

"Yes, I gathered that." Nathaniel has a rueful smile plastered on. "It's nice to meet you."

"You'll be seeing a lot more of me, so if you think you're going to do anything to hurt my girl, you are sadly mistaken." The sword flares on his back, and Nathaniel's eyes widen.

"You carry one of the swords?"

"The Sword of Truth," Dan confirms. "Don't ever make me use it on you."

"I won't. My intent is not to hurt her." He shifts his gaze to me. "Can I speak with you for a moment? Alone?"

I nod, and Dan grudgingly lets me go. "Go talk to Doc and introduce yourself to Mary's crush, Wade."

Dan makes a face. "Yeah, I already

met him."

"I don't like him either," Nathaniel says, his gaze behind me. "He's too whiney."

"Then go meet the Willows. They helped out tonight."

"Sure, but I'm just right over there." Dan shoots Nathaniel one last warning glare and wanders off in the others' direction.

"He's territorial."

"Yeah."

"I'm glad you have someone like him in your life. You need people around you that you can trust. You are special, Emma. There's going to be people who crave what you have, people who will do almost anything to get it. Especially your blood."

"About that…I know you saw what happened with the picture. No one knows I can do that except Dan, my dad, and Silas. No one else. It needs to stay that way."

"I'm not going to tell anyone. It would be signing your death warrant if I did.

That's not a demonic trait, though. Demons can't give life."

"No, it's not," I agree and let it drop. I'm not telling him my real mother was a goddess.

"I lied to you."

"I know."

"You knew?"

This time it's my turn to grin. "You can't lie to a liar, and I'm an expert liar."

He chuckles. "I never thought about it like that."

"I just don't know what you were lying about."

"I came here to steal your gifts. As soon as my grandfather did some digging, I craved your power. My goal was to get you alone and drain your blood and consume your power."

"You had your chance that first night when I passed out."

"I couldn't do it. I thought about it. Really, I did, but every time I started to kill you, something stopped me. I found myself wanting to protect you. The more time I spent with you, the more that feeling grew. You're my sister, and I don't know if the need to protect you sprang up from our familial tie, or if you're just that special, but I'm not going to hurt you, Emma. I won't let anyone else hurt you either."

I can taste the truth of his words on my tongue, but I still don't trust him. Maybe I need time to get to know him, but there is something off. The same kind of weird feeling I get around Doc.

Maybe it's still the foster kid in me who is afraid to let people in.

But I do know one thing.

He is my brother, and I am going to try.

"Okay."

"Just okay?" He quirks a brow at me.

"Just okay. I'm up for getting to know my long-lost brother."

"I'm glad you're willing to give me a chance."

"I saw you a long time ago in a vision of Georgina. She was in a field, and you were four or five, running around, and I was just a baby on a blanket. You know what's weird?"

"What?"

"Georgina called you Jacob."

His eyes widened. "My grandfather said she always called me Jacob while she was pregnant, but my father filled out the birth certificate. I was always Jacob to her, though. She even called me that when she was home over the summer."

Huh.

"I think your crew is getting anxious." Nathaniel nods to where they're all pacing and casting looks our way. "Best we get over there."

I walk back over to everyone, feeling a little better about Nathaniel but determined not to let my unease keep me from getting to know him. I was serious when I told Zeke I'd rather have Nathaniel close where I can watch him than keep him at arm's length and miss something that could get me killed later.

"Can I say it?" Eric is the first person to speak when we reach them.

"Say what?"

He folds his hands together like he's

praying and speaks in the quietest voice I've ever heard him use.

"This house is clean."

We all burst out laughing. Leave it to Eric to cut through the tension with some comedic relief.

"You've been dying to say that since we watched *Poltergeist*."

"You betcha." He grins and slings an arm around me. "I love my freaky friends." He plants a wet one on my cheek. "You da best."

"You're only saying that because I'm the only one who puts up with your lame jokes."

"Hey, now, BFFs over boyfriends!"

Dan rolls his eyes, but I don't miss the indulgent smile. Eric takes some getting used to, but he's growing on Dan.

Wade and his crew are packing up their van and completely ignoring me. That's perfectly fine. I don't like Wade either.

"Caleb was right about you." Cass comes up to us and pulls me into a hug, surprising everyone. "You are a hunter."

"No…"

"Hush that nonsense, *cher*. You're a hunter, and you earned our respect tonight. Any time you need help, you call, and we'll come running."

"I owe you one. So, if you need help, you call me too."

He winks at me then looks over at Dan. "Your man is a holder of one of the swords, yeah?"

I nod.

"Glad you have someone like him watching your back. We'll talk soon, but right now, I'm dead tired and want to sleep for the next week."

"You and me both."

I wave as he, Caryle, and Robert get into their car and drive off, leaving the rest of us to say our goodbyes.

Nathaniel goes back to his hotel, and Wade and his guys leave. Mary frowns after them, but she doesn't look too upset they left without saying goodbye. Well, Ethan said his goodbyes, and he and Eric exchanged numbers. I don't know if that will go anywhere, because Eric struggles with his feelings. He may never be able to embrace them and find a nice girl he can love instead. I just hope he finds happiness.

Doc is the next to leave, saying he'll talk to the Duchaines and assure them their "house is clean." He says it with a straight face. Brownie points to him for that.

Dan has to go straight back to the airport because he can't call in. He's on a homicide. We drop him off at the airport after a very long kiss, which Mary and Eric jump on the second I get back into the car.

I dodge it, not ready to talk about Dan yet. I want to spend some time alone with those feelings first.

That night as I lie in my tiny bed in my dorm room, I have to admit Cass and Nathaniel are right.

I can't hide from my past or my gifts. I can be unhappy, or I can embrace my heritage. Dan loves me no matter what, demonic eyes and all. That means more to me than anything else. Who cares what anyone besides my family thinks of me? I'm not going to hide from The Ghost Girl anymore. I'm going to embrace her and maybe help a few people in the process.

Mary has a few ideas about that. I groan out loud just thinking about it. She wants to start our own YouTube channel about the girl who speaks to ghosts and helps them move on. I told her I was ready to stop hiding from my gifts, but not ready to announce to the world what I can do. She only scoffed at me, and she and Eric started tossing ideas around about the best way to set up our own channel, completely ignoring me and my protests.

I'm not sure showcasing what I do is a good idea. I mean, it's not like I'd be showing off my demonic or god side, but it could open a whole can of worms I'm not equipped to deal with. Then there's my family to consider. Zeke and his parents might have something to say about their only daughter and granddaughter shouting to the world, "I see ghosts." They do have a reputation to uphold. The show might not get any hits at all, though, and then it would be moot.

But what if it did? I know how fascinating the supernatural is to normal people. These and a thousand other concerns rush around in my noggin.

Then there's the whole hunter aspect of my life. Do I want to hunt? I know I kept telling Cass I wasn't a hunter, but even Zeke told me I was one.

It's definitely something to think about.

No matter what I decide to do, life is going to get interesting fast.

And for once, I can't wait.

ACKNOWLEDGEMENTS

When I first started writing the final volume of *The Ghost Files*, I thought to myself, this is it. This is the end of Mattie Hathaway. And I fully intended to let her go, but the fans of the series cried out for more, and after listening to how much Mattie and the gang mattered to so many people, I couldn't let her drift away into a magical dreamland where all finished series characters go.

So, I sat down to start writing this, and the first draft was massive. I started cutting out the junk, and the more I thought about what I wanted for the series, the more I realized if I wanted to do what I intended, writing 70,000-word novels for each book would cause long periods of time between the books. That said, I decided to do shorter novels so I could get them out faster. They're still going to be intense books packed with adventures, new allies, and new enemies. I'll just be able to get them out to you, the reader, faster.

Now, on to the fun part! The thank yous!

First, a big thank you to all *The Ghost Files* readers who demanded more. This series wouldn't exist without you guys.

Next comes Kay C. Steele. She is the best beta reader ever and always so fast to point out what's wrong. She doesn't just tell me it's all rainbows and unicorns. If something's wrong, she'll tell it like it is!

My family deserves a huge shout out for putting up with my muttering and general grumpiness as I worked through this book. They kept me fed and watered and made sure I got some sunshine here and there too.

For Chazz, who doesn't let me go into hermit mode for long. She keeps me from going so deep into my story, I forget everything else. *Gracias, chica*!

For Lori Whitwam, best editor ever. She works with me, gives me extra time when I need it, even when it completely screws her schedule up. Thank you, Lori, I do appreciate you always being willing to work with my hectic, crazy life.

I'm blessed to have so many people in my life who make it possible for me to do the one thing I love to do. I don't know how I'd get by without you all.

From me to all of you, thank you so very much!

Love,
~Apryl Baker

ABOUT THE AUTHOR

So who am I? Well, I'm the crazy girl with an imagination that never shuts up. I LOVE scary movies. My friends laugh at me when I scare myself watching them and tell me to stop watching them, but who doesn't love to get scared? I grew up in a small town nestled in the southern mountains of West Virginia where I spent days roaming around in the woods, climbing trees, and causing general mayhem. Nights I would stay up reading Nancy Drew by flashlight under the covers until my parents yelled at me to go to sleep.

Growing up in a small town, I learned a lot of values and morals, I also learned parents have spies everywhere and there's always someone to tell your mama you were seen kissing a particular boy on a particular day just a little too long. So when you get grounded, what is there left to do? Read! My Aunt Jo gave me my first real romance novel. It was a romance titled "Lord Margrave's

Deception." I remember it fondly. But I also learned I had a deep and abiding love of mysteries and anything paranormal. As I grew up, I started to write just that and would entertain my friends with stories featuring them as main characters.

Now, I live Huntersville, NC where I entertain my niece and nephew and watch the cats get teased by the birds and laugh myself silly when they swoop down and then dive back up just out of reach. The cats start yelling something fierce…lol.

I love books, I love writing books, and I love entertaining people with my silly stories.

Facebook:
https://www.facebook.com/authorAprylBaker

Twitter:
https://twitter.com/AprylBaker

Website:
http://www.aprylbaker.com/

Goodreads:
http://www.goodreads.com/author/show/51736
83.Apryl_Baker

Wattpad:
http://www.wattpad.com/user/AprylBaker7

Newsletter:
https://www.aprylbaker.com/contact

Facebook Fan Page:
https://www.facebook.com/groups/AprylsAngel
s

Instagram:
https://www.instagram.com/apryl.baker

Blog:
https://www.mycrazycornerblog.com/

Amazon:
https://goo.gl/b1br13

Made in the USA
Las Vegas, NV
03 August 2021

27501487R00187